Charlotte Carter

COQ AU VIN

Charlotte Carter is the author of an acclaimed mystery series featuring Nanette Hayes, a young black American jazz musician with a lust for life and a talent for crime solving. Her short fiction has appeared in a number of American and British anthologies. Carter has lived in the American Midwest, North Africa, and France. She currently resides in New York City.

ALSO BY CHARLOTTE CARTER

Walking Bones

THE NANETTE HAYES MYSTERY SERIES

Rhode Island Red
Drumsticks

THE COOK COUNTY MYSTERY SERIES

Jackson Park
Trip Wire

COQ AU VIN

COQ AU VIN

A NANETTE HAYES MYSTERY

Charlotte Carter

VINTAGE CRIME/BLACK LIZARD
Vintage Books
A Division of Penguin Random House LLC
New York

FIRST VINTAGE CRIME/BLACK LIZARD EDITION, AUGUST 2021

Copyright © 1999 by Charlotte Carter

The Library of Congress has cataloged the Mysterious Press edition as follows:
Name: Carter, Charlotte (Charlotte C.).
Title: Coq au vin / Charlotte Carter.
Description: New York : Mysterious Press, 1999.
Identifiers: LCCN 98022565
Subjects: LCSH: African American women—Fiction. | Americans—France—
Fiction. | Women detectives—Fiction. | Paris (France)—Fiction. |
New York (N.Y.)—Fiction. | GSAFD: Detective and mystery stories.
Classification: LCC PS3553.A7736 C6 1999 | DDC 813/.54—dc21
LC record available at https://lccn.loc.gov/98022565

Vintage Crime/Black Lizard Trade Paperback ISBN: 978-0-593-31412-8
eBook ISBN: 978-0-593-31413-5

Book design by Christopher M. Zucker

www.blacklizardcrime.com

Printed in the United States of America
10   9   8   7   6   5   4   3   2   1

For Drew

COQ AU VIN

CHAPTER 1

TRAVELIN' LIGHT

DAMN, I WAS TIRED. My saxophone seemed to weigh more than I did.

I had awakened early that morning and immediately commenced to fill the day with activity—some of it necessary but most of it far from pressing.

I played for a time in midtown, a little north of the theater district; made some nice money. That wasn't my usual stomping ground. I had picked the corner almost at random. I don't know why I did so well. Maybe the people had spring fever, hormones working, calling out for love songs. In fact, the first song I played was "Spring Fever." When you play on the street, you never know why you're a hit or a bust. Is it the mood of the crowd? Is it you? Is it the time of day or the time of year? Anyway, you do the gig and put your money in your belt and move on.

Next, I power walked up to Riverside Park and played there for a while; did my two hours' volunteer work at the soup kitchen on Amsterdam; bought coffee beans at Zabar's; took the IRT downtown; bought a new reed for the sax on Bleecker Street; picked up some paint samples at the hardware store; then played again on lower Park Avenue, closer to my own neighborhood.

Makes me sound like a real flamer, doesn't it? A go-getter, a busy bee. Not true. I'm lazy as hell.

What I was doing was trying to outrun my thoughts. That's what all that busy work was about.

Over dinner the previous night, the b.f. (the shithead's name is Griffin) had announced, number one, he wouldn't be spending the night at my place because he had other plans, and number two, he had other plans . . . period.

I should have known something was up when he said to meet him at the little Belgian café I like in the Village—the other side of town from my place. He hated the food there, but it was convenient for his subway ride home.

This kind of thing has happened to me before. The relationship is at some critical point—or maybe not; maybe it's simply that a certain amount of time has passed and I'm reevaluating it. I meet his family. Mom wants to know if this is "the real thing." I'm asking myself constantly, Is the sex really that good? Should I stay in or should I get out?

And then, a couple of weeks later, before I come to a final decision, he splits.

What's with that?

I always seem to end up asking myself that question. What is with that?

I didn't spend the night crying or anything. I merely came in and stripped out of my clothes and snapped on the radio and finished whatever brown liquor I had in the cabinet. Temper tantrum aside, breaking the porcelain planter in the living-room window had been more of an accident than anything else.

Sleep was a long time coming. But when I awoke in the morning, I just started moving like this—manic.

Now I was exhausted. I packed up my sax and started the short walk to my apartment near Gramercy Park.

Our homeless guy was back. It had been so long since anybody had seen him on the block, we all figured he was dead. But here he was again, in a neck brace, evil as ever, begging for dollars and cussing at anybody with the nerve to give him coins. "Why don't you comb your hair?" he called after me when I stuffed a single into his cup.

I made a quick run to the supermarket and then into the benighted little corner liquor store where a white wine from Chile is the high-end stuff.

I had poured myself a glass, turned on the radio, and read through the mail before I remembered to check the answering machine.

"Nanette, it's me. About tonight. You're still coming over to eat, aren't you? Because I've got something to tell you. It's . . . I'm . . . Well, I'll tell you when you get here. I'm going out now to pick us up some food at Penzler's. You still eat pork, don't you, baby?"

Mom!

Oh shit.

I had forgotten. Two weeks ago I had said maybe we'd have dinner—I walked over to the kitchen calendar—tonight.

I was in no mood to see anybody tonight, let alone Mom, for whom I'd have to put on an act—make out that things were fine between me and Griffin, and that my fabulous—and utterly fictitious—part-time job teaching at NYU was going great. I'd have to be careful never to mention the sax or my street friends or anything remotely connected to my career as an itinerant musician on the streets of Manhattan. She might have been able to handle it if she ever found out that the teaching job was a lie (I was getting steady translation work, at least). But she would have gone absolutely berserk if she knew I blew sax on the street corners with an old fedora turned up to catch the cash. *And* I'd have to haul my ass on the F train out to Queens.

Well, I just wasn't going to make it. Not with all these papers to grade. Not with this pneumonia, cough cough. Not tonight. Tomorrow maybe, but not tonight.

I've got something to tell you.

I turned that gossipy, girlish phrase over in my mind. What was there about that locution that troubled me so? It didn't sound like Mrs. Hayes, that's what. It just did not sound right. And, come to think of it, there was a bit of a quaver in her voice, too.

Oh, God. She's sick. Heart. Cancer.

I rushed to the wall phone and dialed her number. No answer.

I threw my jacket on and locked up.

Halfway to the subway, I realized I was probably being crazy. There were only about three million other reasons my mother might have had to sound worried. Maybe it really was something about her health, but that didn't have to mean that death was knocking on the door.

So why hadn't she answered the phone? She was probably still at Penzler's—Elmhurst's answer to Dean & DeLuca—inspecting the barbecued chickens and braised pork chops and waiting on line for a pound of potato salad. Or out in the backyard. Or over at the Bedlows' house, picking up one of Harriet's cobblers for our dessert.

By then I was at Sixth Avenue. I turned downtown instead of north to the Twenty-third Street station. It was a spur-of-the-moment thing. I had suddenly decided I needed a drink before heading out there, and I needed a little reassuring from the one person whose level head and unfailing equilibrium I could always depend on: my one and only homegirl, Aubrey Davis. Who works as a topless dancer.

We knew early on, at about age nine, that I was the whiz at sight-reading music, inventing lies more believable than the truth, and forging my mother's signature. "Very bright, but a bit unfocused," one of my teachers had told Daddy on parents' night.

Aubrey, however, was the one to call when you wanted to see some dancing. She struggled mightily to teach me one or two moves. But it was no good. I could work the shoulders, and I could usually work the hips, too—just not at the same time. To this day, when I hit the dance floor I look like a holdup man who realizes too late that his victim is carrying a Taser. By the time we were fourteen we'd both thrown in the towel on my dancing career.

It was about that time, on a summer day, that Aubrey's mother abandoned her. She went off to play cards with some people and just never came back. In school, I was the brightest star in the heavens, but Aubrey, when she deigned to join us, was the butt of the kids' pitiless taunting—about her clothes, about her poverty, about her mother, and in time, about her morals. The oddsmakers wouldn't have laid ten cents on Aubrey's chances of getting through life in one piece. They'd have lost. She is a genius at taking care of herself. And my girl never wastes a second looking backward.

Anyway, Aubrey is now one of the bigger draws at Caesar's Go Go Emporium, which is exactly the kind of place it sounds like, tied however circuitously to the mob and located in that one dirty corner of Tribeca where Robert De Niro has not yet bankrolled any émigré restaurateurs.

She performs topless, like I said, and what she wears over

the nasty bits is barely worthy of the term "panties." Between weekly pay and tips she makes a pretty impressive salary, only a fraction of which gets declared to the tax folks. I don't know all the details, but I believe Aubrey has an enviable little portfolio going, thanks to one of her Wall Street admirers. I can always hit her up for money, but I made a vow long ago never to do so unless I was starving. See, if you ask her for a couple hundred, the next thing you know, she's putting down a deposit on a new co-op for you. She is that generous. She is also a great beauty, and I love her madly. So does my mother, who took turns with the other grown-ups in the neighborhood in trying to raise her.

I heard the pounding bass line from halfway up the block. Caesar's. I hate that fucking place. I hate the white men in their middle-management ties who come in for their fix of watery scotch and flaccid titties. I hate the rainbow coalition of construction worker types in their Knicks T-shirts drinking Coors and spending their paychecks on blow jobs. And I've got zero patience with all of them. Not Aubrey, though. She understands men—all kinds of men. And boy, do they love her and her Kraft caramel thighs and her cascades of straightened hair and her voice like warm apple butter.

It is little wonder that Aubrey became a superstar, if you will, at Caesar's. A lot of the other dancers are distracted college girls who'd rather shake their ass in a dive than work behind a cosmetics counter somewhere, or they're strung out on crack and pills. But Aubrey, who isn't even much of a drinker, is focused, engaged, thoroughly there when she's dancing. She has a fierce kind of dedication to her work, and the guys seem to pick up on that immediately. It is the damnedest thing, but they appear to respect her.

There was no one onstage when I walked into the darkened room. The girls were taking a break. I walked double time through the crowd of horny men and had almost made it back to the dressing rooms when I heard a male voice call my name. My whole body stiffened for a few seconds. I kept walking, but the voice rang out again: "Hey, Nan!"

I stopped and turned then. I couldn't believe that any man who actually knew me would not only be hanging in a place like this but would actually want me to *see* him in here.

To my relief, it was only Justin, the club manager. He was standing at the end of the bar, his signature drink, dark rum and tonic, in one hand and one of those preposterously long thin cigarettes in the other. Justin, self-described as "white trash out of Lockport, Indiana," is Aubrey's most ardent fan. Of course, his admiration for her has no sexual dimension.

Justin has a benign contempt for me that actually manifests itself as a kind of affection. I'm just not a femme—his word for a certain kind of lady that he idolizes. (Femmes, you see, are a sub-genre of women in general, all of whom he refers to as "smash-ups.") In any case, he is absolutely right—I am no femme: I don't sleep all day, as Aubrey does, and then emerge after sundown like a vampire; I never paint my nails; I don't own a garter belt or wear spike heels before 9 p.m.; my hair is Joan of Arc short; I don't consider the cadging of drinks one of the lively arts; I don't share his and Aubrey's worship of Luther Vandross; and, probably my worst sin, I cannot shake my booty. The truth is, he thinks I'm overeducated and a secret lesbian. Justin does not understand going to college and does *not* approve of lesbians. But he likes me in spite of himself and, giving the devil his due, he says my breasts are "amazing." We've been out drinking together a couple of times, once just the two of us and once with an old lover of mine, an Irishman who is still turning heads at age forty-two. Yeah, Tom Farrell garnered me quite a few brownie points with Justin. On the other hand, Griffin, my ex, met Justin once, and the two of them scared each other half to death.

I saluted Justin, raising a phantom glass to his health, and continued walking backstage.

Aubrey gave out with one of those Patti LaBelle–register shrieks when she saw me swing through the door. She was busy applying some kind of sparkly shit all over that flawless body and she didn't have stitch one on.

"Christ, Aubrey. Put some clothes on," I said. She made me feel like I had the body of a sumo wrestler and the skin of Godzilla.

"This just makes my night! What are you doing here, sweetheart?" She slipped into a peach-colored robe as she spoke.

"I just thought I'd drop in for a minute on my way out to see Moms. Is there anything to drink back here?"

"Yeah, just a minute." She walked to the door and called out into the ether: "Larry, get me a Jack Daniel's, baby. Tell him don't put no ice in it."

The glass was in my hand almost before I could blink. I took a healthy drink from it.

"You look kind of funny, Nan," she said. "Wait a minute . . . don't tell me that nigger is trifling with you again?"

"No, it's not Griff. It's my mother."

"How is Moms?" she asked me, back at her dressing table.

It was taking me a long time to answer. "What's the matter with her, Nan?"

"Probably nothing," I finally said.

"What does that mean?"

"I know you're going to say I'm crazy, but . . ." I repeated, a bit abashed, the phone message that had set me spinning.

"Nanette, that's exactly what you *are*, girl. How you know it ain't something good instead of something terrible? She could be getting married again for all you know."

"Aubrey, I know you're a relentless optimist. But give me a break, huh. Moms is getting married? To who?"

"How do I know that?"

"Or me, for that matter."

"That's what I'm saying, Nan. You don't know all her business."

I took another deep drink of the bourbon. "Trust me, it's not wedding news."

"Okay, fool. She's not getting married. But that still don't mean she got cancer, do it?"

"No, you're right, it doesn't. But I'm still a little freaked. Which brings me to the reason—another reason—I came here. I thought if you could get a couple of hours off tonight, maybe you'd go out there with me."

"Oh shit. I can't, baby. I *am* taking some time off tonight— but I gotta meet somebody for a couple of hours."

"Oh." It flitted through my mind to ask who she was meeting, but then I remembered myself, and who I was talking to, and who she worked for. I didn't want to know any of the particulars. Of course, it might have been something perfectly innocent, but I thought I'd better let it go.

I stayed a few minutes longer, until it was almost time for her to go on again. She insisted on having one of the guys run me out to Queens in his car. I ran through my head the possibility of staring at the thick neck of some club gofer while I sat in the back seat all the way across town and then over the Long Island Expressway to Elmhurst. Or maybe, I thought with a shudder, he might try to chat me up. We'd talk about— what?—Heavy D's latest, or some new designer drug? My heart sank.

Then I mentally put myself on the subway, stop after stop after stop. I didn't even have a newspaper to distract me.

I went for the car.

I left with the promise that I would call her the next day to give her a full report on Mom's news, whatever it turned out to be.

On the way out I ran into Justin.

"What's happening, Smash-up?"

"Same old, same old, Justin. You know."

"Have a quick one with me, girlfriend."

"I can't."

"Got a date?"

"Yep. Dinner. With my mother."

"Ooooh. Bring me back some cornbread."

I guffawed. He didn't know how funny that was.

THE KITCHEN WAS SPOTLESS, as always. But then, why shouldn't it be? Mom never cooked. Everything was takeout or premixed or delivered in stay-warm aluminum foil.

"Mom, I'm here! Where are you?"

My mother's cotton dress was as surreal as the kitchen counters in its neatness. Decorous pageboy wig bobby-pinned in place. Makeup specially blended by one of the black salesladies at the Macy's in the mall.

It must be eight, nine years now since Daddy left her. But if I no longer remembered the exact date that had happened, Mom sure did. I bet she could tell you what she'd eaten for breakfast that day, what shoes Daddy was wearing when he broke the news to her. On those rare occasions when Mom talks about him, she never uses his name, referring to my father only as "him."

My father soon remarried: a young white teacher on his staff at the private school where he is now the principal. Outside of the occasional birthday lunch, Christmastime, and so on, I saw very little of him. He was happy enough, I suppose, in his new life. And he never missed an alimony payment.

"Nanette, what have you got on your feet?"

"They're called boots, Mother."

"Those things are something you wear down in the basement when you're looking to kill a rat. Don't tell me you dress like that for—"

"Holy mackerel, Mother, what is it you have to tell me!"

"It's about Vivian," she said grimly.

I fell into a chair, suddenly exhausted. No melanoma. Thank God. No wedding.

Vivian, my father's sister, had been my idol when I was a kid. Breezing into town and swooping me up, Aunt Vivian meant trips into Manhattan and eating exotic food and hanging with her hip friends and my first sip of beer and every other cool thing you can imagine when you're ten years old and your father's baby sister is a sophisticated sometime-fashion-model who drinks at piano bars and parties with people who actually make the rock 'n' roll records you hear on the radio.

My father felt about his little sister Vivian the way Justin feels about lesbians. He disapproved of her friends and her nomadic ways and her prodigious consumption of vodka and her way-out hairdos and everything else about her lifestyle, which he didn't understand at all.

My mother didn't understand it any better than he did, but she loved Vivian just the same. Maybe that was due to the same kind of sympathy with strays that had moved her to take Aubrey to her heart. Mom looked on with pity while Auntie Viv blew all her money and drank too much and got her heart broken by trifling pretty men and then recovered to start the cycle all over again.

In time Vivian married and divorced—two or three times, if I remember right—and moved out of New York and then back again, half a dozen times—to L.A. and Mexico and France and Portugal—wherever the job or the party or the boyfriend might take her. Daddy and she finally had one final royal blowup

during the cocaine-laced eighties and stopped speaking to each
other altogether. We didn't even know where she had been living
for the past eight or ten years.

And now, apparently, some disaster had befallen her.

"Is she dead?" I asked. "How did it happen?"

"No, no. She isn't dead."

"She isn't? Then what happened to her? What about Vivian?"

"She's in trouble. Wait here a minute."

Mom vanished into the dining room.

I sat looking around the kitchen in puzzlement, at last fixing
on the covered Styrofoam plates that held our dinner, waiting to
be popped into the microwave. And I thought the day had been
long and weird *before* I crossed the bridge into Queens. What the
hell was going on here?

"Look at these."

She handed me two pieces, one a standard tourist postcard
with a corny photo of the Eiffel Tower, the other a telegram.

I turned the postcard over and read:

> *Long time No see. Hate to ask you but I'm strapped. Can
> you spare anything? Just send what you can—if you
> can. Love, Viv.*

The postmark on the card was about three weeks old.

There was an address beneath her signature. A place on the
rue du Cardinal Lemoine—my Lord, Viv was in Paris.

I looked up at Mom and began to ask a question, but she
ordered me to read the telegram first, which was dated a week or
so after the postcard.

JEAN
DID YOU GET MY CARD?

WORSE. I CAN'T GET OUT.
VIV.

"What's this about?" I asked, the fear rising in my voice.

"I don't know, honey. I don't know." Her spine stiffened then, and her eyes took on a glassy look. "I finally called . . . *him.* I mean, he is her brother."

"You're kidding! You called Daddy?"

She nodded.

I tried to imagine white Mrs. Daddy picking up the phone in their apartment near Lincoln Center. Handing the receiver over. Jesus, the look on his face when she told him who it was.

"What did he say?" I asked. "Did Viv write to him, too?"

"Yes. But he doesn't want to know anything about Vivian. Says he tore the card up without reading it. It's a sin. I told him I hoped one day he would be hurting in the same way and when he reached out for help—well, never mind. I told him I think it's a sin, that's all."

I shook my head. "Wow. This is so weird. What are you going to do? You don't have any money to send her, and if Pop won't do it—"

"He wouldn't give it to her, but I managed to shame him into giving me something for you."

"*Me?* What do you mean?"

She pulled out a chair for herself then and sat down in it before answering. "Listen, Nan."

"What?"

"*I* don't have any money to spare. But—well, I do have it, but it's not mine. As a matter of fact it's Vivian's money."

"What are you talking about, Mother?"

"I mean I actually do have some money for Vivian—especially for her. When your grandfather died, he left most of what he had to your daddy, naturally. And you got enough to take that beautiful trip. But you know how he was. He feuded with Viv just like your father did, but at the end he wanted to come to some kind of peace with her. Nobody even knew where Vivian was at the time. So he left her some money and gave it to me to keep for her. It's in a special account. Waiting. There must be close to ten thousand in it by now."

"Ten thousand dollars. That sure sounds like enough to bail her out of trouble. And you mean you've had this money all along?"

"Yes. I knew sooner or later we'd hear from her again."

"But not like this," I said.

"No. Not like this. And so . . ." She glanced away from me then.

"What is it?"

"I know it's a lot to ask, Nan. You haven't seen Viv since you were a kid. I just know she's over there drinking, broke, stranded somewhere. Maybe even sick. I wouldn't know where to begin to help her. I don't know how I'd even get out of the airport over there. But I thought—since you've been there so many times—I thought maybe you could go over there and help her— take this money to her and help her get home. Like I said, I managed to shame your father into giving me enough for your expenses."

Expenses?

"What are you saying, Mother? You want me to go to Paris?"

"Yes. Would you do it? If—I mean, only if you could take the time from work. You're going to be on spring vacation soon, aren't you?"

"It started yesterday, Mom. No problem."

A lot to ask! *Holy*—

I felt a kick right then. Right on the shin. I knew who that was: my conscience, Ernestine. I just kicked the bitch right back. Yes, I'm a liar, I told her, a deceiver, a coldhearted Air France slut. I was thinking not of my aunt Viv in a French drunk tank but of the braised rabbit in that bistro on the rue Monsieur-le-Prince.

A lot to ask? Coq au vin, here I come!

CHAPTER 2

CAN'T WE BE FRIENDS?

I KNOW I'M A FOOL. A sentimentalist. A sucker for a sad song. The same old hokey things undo me every time.

I was crying so hard I could barely see out the window of the taxi, one of those workhorse Renaults with a driver who smoked Gitanes, a beautifully dappled Dalmatian asleep beside him on the front seat. It was April and the trees were budding and we had just passed the Arc de Triomphe and it was tearing my heart out.

It helped a lot that I had sucked down about fifty glasses of Veuve Clicquot on the flight over and been hit on big-time by both an African diplomat in a vintage Armani and a sublimely big-nosed Frenchman.

Drying my eyes, I recalled that first time I saw Paris, from the window of a train. I was still a student and traveling on the cheap. I took a charter flight into Amsterdam, where I met up with a couple of classmates and their European boyfriends. After a couple of days of museum-going and smoking pot till I was pixelated, I took the train into Paris. That first sight of the roof of the Gare du Nord, alive with pigeons, had produced the same kind of waterworks.

By the time the cab deposited me at the picturesque little square in the 5th arrondissement, I was working on one hell of a hangover. The address on Vivian's postcard turned out to be a clean but decidedly unglamorous little hotel at the top of a rise in the pavement. Their one-star rating was not mere modesty— nothing fancy about the place. I set my valise down and walked over to *reception.*

There was no such American madame as Vivian Hayes registered at the hotel, the well-fed gentleman behind the desk reported. Perhaps my friend was at the small hotel at the other end of the square? No, I said, checking the postcard again, this was the address given. It occurred to me then that Aunt Viv might be using either of two—or was it three?—married names. So I began to describe her, thinking even as I did so that she had probably changed so much since our last meeting that the description might be worthless. I was just about to dig into my bag for a twenty-year-old snapshot of Vivian when the monsieur suddenly realized who I was seeking.

A sneer pulled at his lips. "Oh yes. I recall your friend now." I waited for him to go on. "This Madame Hayes," he said contemptuously, had checked out more than ten days ago.

"Checked out" was not exactly the phrase he used to describe her departure. Apparently Vivian had left without paying the last week's rent, abandoning her suitcase and clothing and personal items. She had simply gone out one afternoon and never returned.

Not good.

I had counted on some kind of trouble. Still, I didn't have to hit the panic button yet. I might have to mount a search for her. On the other hand, she might be able to raise a few dollars from somewhere, in which case she would show up again to pay her bill and collect her things.

But I couldn't think about that at the moment. My head was pounding and I needed some sleep—real sleep, not airplane nodding. This hotel was not exactly what I'd had in mind as a base of operations, but it would do for now. Hell, dowdy French hotels short on amenities but rich in character had been the sites of some of my most delightful adventures.

I asked for a room and, to forestall any problems, paid for a few days in advance. I pulled the envelope with the Thomas Cook money orders earmarked for Aunt Vivian out of my carry-on bag and committed it to the hotel safe. Mom had asked if it wouldn't be better to buy traveler's checks in my own name, but I wanted to guarantee I wouldn't be tempted to start dipping into those funds for my own use. In Vivian's place, I don't think I would've appreciated any messenger messing about with my inheritance, even if it was a totally unexpected gift from heaven.

I splurged on the best room in the house. Even so, the toilet was down the hall. The bidet had been cracked and repaired half a dozen times. The bureau smelled faintly of mildew. But the room was a good size, and the view wasn't bad. Not bad at all: my room, on the sixth floor, looked out over the busy square with its ancient copper fountain. I put in five minutes at the open window just looking at the people, pulling the air into my chest—and thinking about Aunt Vivian, somewhere out there. I didn't know yet what kind of shape I'd find her in. But I did know she wouldn't be high stepping in her designer jeans and smart black pumps. She wouldn't be laughing her tantalizing laugh that put lights in her clear brown eyes. She wouldn't be young anymore.

I thought, too, of my first trip to Paris and all the subsequent ones; of the friends I'd once had here, all dispersed to other places, other lives, now; of my summer in Provence; of the meals, the men, the just plain fun. I'd been happy, ecstatic, in Paris—drunk on it—and yet I'd also known that peculiar *tristesse* that could fasten around your heart like a vise, for no particular reason, and suddenly make you feel so very alone.

Tiredness overtook me then. I closed the shutters tight. I turned back the covers on the creaky iron bed and slipped between the ironed white sheets. And then—darkness.

THE TRICK is not to let yourself sleep too long lest you fall victim to jet lag. It was the only travel tip I could ever remember. You've got to crash and allow the old ankles to lose the swelling that results from sitting constricted in one place for so long. Nap, yes. But you mustn't sleep too long, or you'll be on the way back home before your body clock is running right again.

I was groggy when I pulled myself out of dreamland—and ravenous. I opened the metal shutters. *Pam!* Night had fallen. Those inimitable lights were all around me, and, down below, the canopies of a thousand cafés. I went and cleaned up quickly in the communal shower room and then jumped into a leotard and some black trousers. I threw my long raincoat over that and I was ready to roll.

I did a quick turn around the Pantheon, where I had often gone in the dark of night to sit and think and sometimes consume a couple of *boules* of rich ice cream purchased at one of the carts dotting the landscape. Then I headed back across the square and the boulevard Saint-Michel, pulsating with young people.

I hit boulevard Saint-Germain, or rather it hit me. It was Friday night and the street was hopping. Traffic was the predictable nightmare. I took a deep breath and ran, snaked, bullied my way across the street, heedless of the color of the traffic lights. I headed north then, away from the worst of the crowds. I had decided to eat at the Café Cloche, which was on the pricey side, but my mouth was watering for a couple of their beautiful spring lamb chops. I remembered that they didn't take reservations—the only reason I had for believing I'd get a table on a Friday night. The cross streets were beginning to look familiar now. Yes, this was the block. The café was near.

Except it wasn't. It was not there. The Café Cloche, where I'd once been seduced by a chain-smoking academic from Toulouse over a fine *daube* of beef, was no more. I stared stupidly, dejected, at the darkened window of the boutique that had replaced the restaurant.

Well, what was the big deal? Things change. So I'd find someplace else to eat dinner. A restaurant closing was a small thing, yet, inexplicably, it unsettled me. I walked back slowly into the heart of the crowd and found a friendly-looking if undistinguished place where I ordered foie gras and then went on to langoustines and a half bottle of white wine. Afterward, I browsed somnolently through a few of the late-night bookstores on Saint-Michel, buying nothing, and found my way back to the hotel.

I got into my nightgown almost immediately. It was cool in the room, but I opened the window wide and let the low night sky fall in on me. Another one of those singular Paris moments. The lights on the Pantheon were silver blue and I watched them for a long time, wondering how many others were doing the same thing, their hearts moving in their chest. But, curiously enough, I had stopped crying.

I MADE A BET WITH MYSELF as I called downstairs to order breakfast. At every hotel I'd ever lived in on this side of the Seine, the maid's name was Josette. I figured that would never change.

I lost. Marise bid me good morning in her musical colonial accent—Was she from Antigua? Maybe Saint Croix?—and set the wooden tray bearing my soupy black coffee and croissants down at the foot of the bed.

I spent the late morning and all afternoon checking out the really low-rent hotels on streets like Gay-Lussac, thinking that Vivian might have got her hands on a few bucks to live on, but not enough to go back to the hotel in the Square. The next day, I figured, I'd go another rung down the ladder and try Pigalle and the parts of Bastille that had not yet been gentrified. Then, if I didn't turn up any leads, I'd head out to the edge of the city, rue Whatever, where I'd probably be mugged and left for dead.

I put in a full day. Nothing. At six o'clock I returned to the hotel and put in a call to my mother, reporting on my progress, or rather lack of progress.

I took a long soak in the pay-per bathroom down the hall and changed into something slightly slinky. There was a fabulous wine bar on the rue du Cherche-Midi that I loved.

They sold lighting fixtures there now. I stood on the pavement watching the clerk clear the register and begin to close up for the evening. I could have cried.

I wandered down into the Métro and took the train to Pont Marie, on the Right Bank. Surely the much more staid wine bar that a friend's father had once taken us to would still be there. And it was. But it was obvious there would be no light-hearted seductions taking place that evening. Oh no. No sharing *un steak frites* with a cute translator and then a nightcap at some avant-garde jazz loft. No and no. Average age of the patrons at this stately establishment: fifty-five by my calculations. Successful businessmen and their coworkers, or their Chanel-clad ladies. I put away two lovely glasses of Medoc and was on my way.

I walked along the Seine in the twilight, feet hurting in my strappy heels. The magazine/postcards/junk stands on the quai were all closed now. Here and there I could hear voices down below, along the water. I had to smile. One thing you never forget, your first kiss on the banks of the Seine. I just know it's one of those pictures that go flying across your vision as you lay dying.

I had had nothing to eat except the breakfast croissant and a yogurt taken on the run midday. I was starving, but I hated the thought of eating alone again.

What choice did I have, though? I went to Au Pactole, a perfectly nice place on Saint-Germain, just the tiniest bit stuffy, up the block from a hotel I'd once lived in—the Hotel de Lima. It was almost pleasurable to behave so formally with the maître d', like playing a role or wearing a disguise. *Hmm—she is black and French-speaking. Must be an immigrant. Spinster on vacation from the provinces,* I could almost hear the young waiter thinking. *Trying to dress Parisian. Not bad looking. Needs to get laid, though.* I was the only solo table in the good-sized room, which was awash in fresh white flowers and skyscraper-tall candles. After an already-too-heavy meal, I pigged on cheese and a big-time dessert.

The thing is, I mused during my meandering walk home along the quai, the main thing is: the police have to be avoided.

If nothing happened with my search for Vivian in the next day or so, I might have to contact the American embassy. But not the French police. It was half instinctual cop-o-phobia and half worry that maybe Vivian had wandered into something not on the up-and-up; then there was the plain gut-clenching terror based on the Gallic mindset. Guilty until proven innocent was not a metaphor over here. You just did not fuck with cops in this country—not even traffic cops.

What does a foreigner do when he or she is broke, in trouble—no friends, no resources? I didn't know. True, I had bummed around Europe before, hitchhiked with companions, smoked dope with kids I met at discos, and so on. But I had never been anything like stranded or in trouble with the law. I always had a return ticket in my pocket, and help was a collect call away. I thought about the asshole white boys who thought they were slick enough to get away with smuggling hashish out of Turkey. I found myself shuddering.

The Herald Tribune? What about placing an ad there? "Aunt Viv: You're richer than you think. Call home. All is forgiven." Something to that effect.

Not a likely venue. Vivian had lived in Paris before. She had enough French that if she read the newspapers at all, she'd read a French one.

I was at the Pont Neuf. Shit, I had been so lost in my thoughts that I'd overshot the hotel. I was beat, my toes crying out for release.

Give me your tired, your poor . . . your Manolo Blahniks . . . your tarte tatin.

Not just tired now. I was slappy. Maybe I hadn't escaped the jet lag after all. I stood on the quai for a few minutes more. Well, good night, old Notre-Dame. And if it's not too much trouble, help me find Aunt Viv before I have to go to the 19th. Amen.

I VISITED AT LEAST FIFTEEN fleabag hotels and hostels the next day. I was seeing the side of Paris they don't print up on the picture postcards. The homeless, the druggies, the bag ladies were nowhere near as numerous, as filthy, or as desperate as their New York cousins, but they did nothing for tourism, either.

Just to make myself feel less like a mendicant, I went and had lunch in an overpriced, overdecorated restaurant in Montmartre and then took the funicular up to Sacré-Cœur. I looked out over the city while the shutterbugs swarmed all around me. Maybe there is a heaven, I thought, and it's nothing more than these rooftops.

As long as I was doing the American in Paris bit, I figured I'd go to American Express, on the very remote chance that Vivian had left a message there. Of course, she'd have to know I was in Paris. But what did I have to lose? Perhaps she had spoken to my mother by now.

No such luck. And now I was stuck in the busy 8th, clogged with crazed shoppers and sightseers, the traffic like a million killer bees. I had to admit, the Opéra was looking a great deal spiffier than the last time I'd been in Paris. Choking on exhaust and too weary to do any window-shopping of my own, I zigzagged across the boulevard des Capucines and went down into the Métro station.

Home at last, thank the baby Jesus. The alert, generous-bosomed madame who seemed to rule at the hotel was having her afternoon *tisane* when I stopped at the desk for my key. I must have looked about as frazzled as I felt, because she offered me a cup.

French businesswomen are about the least homey human beings imaginable. Anybody would be scared of them. I know I am. This one, however, told me she had noticed my saxophone, and wondered if I was in Paris to play an engagement somewhere. She had always admired *le jazz*, she said, and at the time of their wedding anniversary each year, she and her husband enjoyed making an evening of it at the music club just off Saint-Germain-des-Prés. You know—the one with the likeness of Satchmo in black plaster in the entryway.

I told the madame, in as little detail as possible, about my search for Aunt Viv. She was sympathetic—genuinely so, I believed—and when she offered further assistance, I jumped on it.

The madame's husband relieved her at the desk while the two of us climbed into the taxi she had ordered. We were going to La

Pitié Salpêtrière, a giant medical complex in the 13th arrondissement that also housed the city morgue. It made sense, didn't it,
to check there first? Oh yes, it was quite sensible, my companion
agreed. After all, if, heaven forbid, Vivian was at La Pitié, then
there was little point in canvassing the hospitals and the emergency rooms and hospices and so on—our search would be over.

The office where we waited had a beautiful view of the Jardin
des Plantes. As the lady from the administrative office led us
along the corridors, the worst kinds of morbid one-liners were
running through my brain. I couldn't help it. It was like whis-
tling in the graveyard.

Back in the fresh air, I went weak with relief, happy to know
that Viv was not one of the bodies in those human filing cabi-
nets. The madame and I rested for a few moments on a bench in
the Jardin des Plantes and then caught another cab home.

Back at the hotel we worked out a fair way of computing the
phone charges I was racking up calling the appropriate municipal offices to determine if anyone fitting my aunt's general description had been admitted to a Paris hospital. It seemed only right,
I told her gratefully, that I also pay the week's rent that my
aunt had skipped on. That was most responsible of me, she said.
Would I like to pay that now, or should she add that sum to my
own bill at the end of my stay?

None of the hospitals had any mysterious amnesiacs in resi-
dence who might be my poor aunt. So, as far as we knew, Aunt
Vivian was still alive, somewhere out there. She had to be. If she
was broke, how was she going to get out of Paris? I was going
to have to bite the bullet and go to the embassy soon, it seemed.

It was time for me to clear out of Madame's way and let her
get her dinner started. I thanked her for all her efforts—the tea
and sympathy not the least of them—and went upstairs.

About seven o'clock I put on a fresh shirt and jeans and left
the hotel, with no particular destination.

I wound up at one of the revival cinemas near the place every-body referred to as the Beat Hotel, a dump with character over on the rue Gît-le-Cœur, which I had checked out the previous day. Its reputation had been made by William Burroughs and his crowd in the fifties, and I guess its legend was still going strong. Not a single vacancy.

The street was clogged with kids of all nations, hanging out, playing guitars, smoking reefer, dry humping in doorways, eating *frites* and souvlaki, and just glorying in being alive and young and stupid.

At least the movie was no disappointment. How many times had I seen *Children of Paradise* since my college roommate and I first caught it on campus? Too many to count. I cried again anyway.

Lord, what a beautiful night. There was no way I was going to dinner alone again. Maybe I should turn into the first bar I saw and make a fool of myself by begging some stranger to come eat with me—or perhaps I should just pick up a sandwich someplace and call it a night.

I went for the sandwich. I would not have been good company for anybody.

AFTER COFFEE the next morning an idea came to me. No, I hadn't yet thought of my next move for locating Vivian. It was some-thing a lot goofier than that.

In fact, it was probably about the goofiest idea that had ever come my way: I decided to take my sax down into the Métro and play for change. Reckless. Silly. Ill-considered. Preposterous.

Formidable. I'd do it.

It was the stuff of fantasy. Maybe I didn't have the chops a lot of my fellow street musicians back in Manhattan had, but at least

I'd be able to say I played in Paris. I got cleaned up and dressed in a hurry. I wanted to get out of the room and down into the Métro before I had a chance to wimp out.

I got a polite *bonjour* along with an indulgent smile from the old monsieur behind the reception desk as I tripped past him, my instrument case festooned with an old India print scarf I often use as a strap for the sax.

I bought a booklet of Métro tickets and passed through the turnstile. It was an act of supreme hubris to set up shop at Odéon, one of the busier stops in the city. What with the number of hip Parisians who lived in or passed through the neighborhood every day—students, intellectuals, musicians, jazzaholics of all stripes—I was betting half of them had heard better horns than mine before they'd finished their morning coffee.

But what the hell. I wasn't playing to pay the rent; I was living out a fantasy. I settled myself at the mouth of the passageway connecting the Clignancourt line to the Austerlitz, took a deep breath, and started to blow. I began with "How Deep Is the Ocean." Hardly anyone took notice of me. That was okay, because my playing was a lot rustier than my French. I didn't sound so great.

Still, I pressed on. I chose "With a Song in My Heart" next. Not bad, if I do say so myself. And indeed, a cool-looking man in an expensive trench coat stood there attentively until I'd finished, and then began to dig into his pocket for change. The sound of the francs hitting the bottom of the case made my heart soar. I gave the guy a big shit-eating grin and immediately launched into "Lover Man." I felt so good, anything seemed possible. Maybe even a certifiable miracle. Maybe I'd see Viv hurrying along the tunnel, running to catch a train.

The late-morning crowd was replaced by the noontime one, people bustling along to lunch appointments, or going to do their shopping, or heading home for a leisurely meal and maybe some quick nooky—or vice versa—before returning to work.

I had to chuckle at the idea I'd had earlier in the morning—that if I kept at it all day, maybe I could make enough in tips to buy Moms and Aubrey some nice perfume. Ha. What I made was maybe enough to take a whiff of some Chanel. It really didn't bother me, though. I was having a good time.

I went aboveground about two o'clock and found a cart that had nice-looking crêpes. I strolled along the Seine as I ate, and then turned into a beautiful old *tabac* on the Quai Voltaire, where I had a *grand café* and bummed a cigarette from a waiter who was tall enough for the NBA and weighed about ten pounds.

I couldn't wait to get back to my post in the subway. And when I did, I hit the ground running. I had never managed to make "It Never Entered My Mind" sound like that before in my life. And my "On Green Dolphin Street" ran a close second. I even got a nice round of applause from a group of older women with folding umbrellas.

Don't ever get too comfortable. It's just one of a thousand lessons that I have never truly taken in. My mother has been cautioning me about it since I was old enough to crawl. And Ernestine, my conscience, never tires of saying it. Yet I always forget.

It was about five-thirty. I got through a couple of bars of "You Took Advantage of Me" before I realized something strange was up. I was hearing the same licks being played—note for note—not twenty feet away. On a violin, of all things. It startled the shit out of me. In fact, for a moment I thought I was hallucinating. I looked into the passageway and saw a long-legged, light-skinned black man with demure dreadlocks and wire-rim spectacles gazing directly, defiantly into my eyes while he bowed absent-mindedly.

I stood where I was, seething, until he finished, and then

strode over to the gangly Caribbean-looking prick. "What the fuck do you think you're doing? I was here first," I told him in rapid-fire French.

His eyes bugged behind the glass of his spectacles.

"*Idiot!*" I shouted at him. And then went on to ask him if he was deaf, and then if he was under the mistaken impression that he was funny. I finished with "Who the hell do you think you are—Marcel Marceau?"

There was plenty of anger in his eyes, but he said nothing. Which only increased my fury.

"*Eh bien, salaud? Pourquoi tu me reponds pas?*"

"I'm not answering you," he said, acidly, and in English, "because I don't know any gutter French yet."

"Oh my God. You're . . . an American."

At this point he chose to answer me in French, adding a smirk to his little repertory of expressions: "No need to be so snotty about it. So are you—obviously."

"Obviously?" I began to splutter. "Oh, so *I* don't know how to speak French? Is that what that lame remark is supposed to mean?"

More smirk.

I got right up in his face then. "Don't even think about criticizing my accent, mister. You speak French like a pig."

"That's because I am an autodidact. I hope to polish my accent while—"

"An *au-to-di-dact*," I repeated, followed by scornful laughter. I was being the schoolyard bully picking on the kid with the bulging book bag. It was cheap and unworthy of me, but I couldn't put the brakes on it. "Unbelievable. I have to come all the way to Paris to deal with an evil, pretentious, bourgeois asshole from the hood—"

"I was thinking the same thing about you."

"Hey, you see here! I may be pretentious, but I am *not* bourgeois—and I sure as hell am not from *your* hood."

"You can be from Jupiter for all I care," he said, abruptly ending our absurd argument. "Just as long as you move along. This is my spot."

"What do you mean, your spot? You own it or something?"

"I mean I got a right to play here at this time four days a week. I have a piece of paper that says so."

"I don't believe you."

"I have no interest in what you believe. I'm a legal resident of the city of Paris and I have an artist permit to play here."

I was going to slice into him some more, but suddenly all the wind was gone from my sails. Suddenly I knew who I reminded myself of: a monster-gold-earring-wearing gangsta girl; hunching her shoulders, threatening, using her high-polished fingernails like a garden trowel as she read out some enemy in subliterate English.

"You know what?" I said, calm now. "You can die on this fucking spot, mister legal resident. Forget you."

I turned on my heel and walked back to my case.

As I climbed the stair at the other end of the tunnel, I could hear him playing "How About You?"

His playing was effortless, swinging, like something humming inside your own head.

I'd like to show you some New York in June, I thought bitterly.

Oh, but shit, he was good.

WELL, that was nice and ugly.

"Ugly" didn't really capture the essence of it, though. It was, to use some prissy language of my own, mortifying. Jesus—why did I do that!

I hated myself.

Aboveground again, my face burned with shame. Two black Americans, strangers, meeting in Paris under those singularly strange circumstances—it should have been an occasion for rejoicing. But what do we do? Rather, what do I do? Ridicule. Curse. Clown. Fight over a little patch of pee-soaked concrete. It was horrible. And the more I thought about it, the more thoroughly depressed I became.

I walked for a while, trying to get myself in hand, shake off the bad feelings. I sat in the Jardin du Luxembourg for a little while, smelling the sweetness of the grass, despising it. I watched the parents as they sauntered home with their kids; the lovers as they kissed in parting. Everybody seemed to be carrying a baguette for that night's dinner. Man, it would be so nice to be invited to somebody's house for dinner. I was yearning for somebody just to call me by my name—for something familiar like that. A plain meal in an apartment I'd visited many times, and a couple of hours of aimless, civilized conversation. I am still civilized, I told myself. Despite that appalling interlude in the Métro. I'm not the asshole who behaved that way. I'm better than that—really.

I went and had a drink at the Café de Flore. In fact, I had a few of them.

Like every musician, probably, I had often wondered what it was like to play high on drugs. All the cornball stuff crosses your mind: does the heroin unlock some door in your soul? Does it make you better? I don't just mean does it make you play better. I mean, are *you* better, however briefly. Does it really make the pain go away? The daily pain. The centuries of pain.

And what were we going to do if suddenly it all did go away? Would we even know who we were anymore?

The waiter was looking at me, the bottle in his left hand, the smile on his lips like a question mark.

I shook my head. No more, *merci*.

I wasn't exactly merry, but I'd had enough wine to make me lighten up somewhat. Enough with the clichés, Nan, I cautioned myself. No more being blue in Paris. Gotta lose that "Azure-tay," as Nat Cole sang.

So, back to work. I walked for a few blocks and then descended into the station called Saint-Sulpice. The crowds had disappeared. I set up and began to play again. Not many passersby, but what did it matter? The sounds of my horn ricocheted hauntingly off the tiled walls. I felt almost as though I was in my own private city, the occasional visitor dropping a few francs into my case like a toll to enter the gates.

I played "Something to Live For" and another Ellington, "Come Sunday."

I think what happened was, I pushed it too far. One minute I was playing the break on "Ill Wind," my eyes closed, and the next moment I was seeing stars. I had thought I heard a kind of scuffling noise farther down the tunnel, but I was so wrapped up in playing I paid no attention.

All I know is that suddenly they were on me: two white guys in denim and swastika-ed leather, short haircuts, bad teeth. And one of them was banging my head against the tiles.

I began to flail around, hit out blindly, but my fists never connected with anything. I became dimly aware of shouting—somewhere far off—and then I heard a ripping sound. They were tearing the pockets off my jeans, going after my money, I guess. The instrument case must have gotten overturned, because the few coins that had been inside it I heard rolling up the tunnel floor. Someone was pulling at the strap of the sax now, but it was all twisted around my head. I heard the unmistakable epithet, *negre*, spoken through clenched teeth as I took a blow to the face. I once saw a film clip of Thelonious Monk playing at the Five Spot in New York. When the spirit moved him, he got up from the piano and spun himself around madly, like a holy drunk. That's how I felt right then, as if someone had set me spinning and I was never going to stop.

My head and heart were drumming hard. I raised my hands to cover my ears. Something on my face. Something on my hands. Wet. That was blood. Was I cut up?

So this is how it ends, I thought. Me beaten to death by skinheads. Aunt Viv starves to death in a back alley or rots in prison. Mother, grief stricken, carted off screaming to the insane asylum. Daddy, riddled with guilt, commits suicide. Now *that* is what I call Negro angst.

One of them is coming back to finish me off now. His face comes into focus. Wish I had the strength to kick him in the balls.

But wait—it's not a white face. And this guy's got a mop of curly hair and wears glasses.

And, somehow, all the noise has stopped.

CHAPTER 3

I DIDN'T KNOW ABOUT YOU

WHITE SHEETS. Creaky bedsprings. My old suitcase open on top of the bureau. Unless heaven, or hell, was a budget hotel room with no TV, I was still alive.

Oh yes. There was something else in my room that tipped me off I wasn't dead: a fine-looking, long-legged, high-yellow black man, snoring softly, sitting on a hard chair, his big bare feet propped up at the foot of my bed. He wasn't wearing any pants. Gray T-shirt over matching briefs.

Lord-a-muzzy, I am still alive.

"How's it going, sleeping beauty?"

Shit. He caught me staring at his shorts. How gross.

"I'm okay, I think. My nose hurts a little. Is it broken?"

"Nothing broken far as I can tell," he said.

There followed a long and awkward silence.

"Last night's still fuzzy to you, I guess," he said, yawning and getting to his feet. He reached for his trousers and turned his back while he zipped up. "I asked if you wanted to go to the hospital, but you wouldn't do it."

"Yeah, one member of the family in trouble is enough," I mumbled.

"What?"

"Doesn't matter. I remember now. You rescued me."

He didn't respond. Instead, he went over to the basin and began to splash water on his face.

"Damn nice of you," I said, laughing a bit, too embarrassed to do much else. "After that scene I pulled—going out on you like that in the Métro—you should have let them kill me."

He shook his head. "Forget it."

"God, I haven't even asked, how are you? Mister black white knight. There were two of those freaks. Did they hurt you?"

"Not really. I'm not much of a hero. I was screaming like a white lady and three or four other folks came running to help us out. The Aryan League didn't even manage to get your wallet."

I suddenly buried my face in my hands and moaned.

"What is it?" he said, alarmed. "Headache?"

"No, no, no. I'm just cursing my fucking karma. I don't know why I'm so surprised when stuff like this happens to me. You know what I mean?"

"Uh—not really."

"What's the story downstairs, by the way? Did you bring me in here all bloody and stuff? And what did they say—'Be out by tomorrow morning'?"

"I told them I witnessed two thugs trying to rob you. The madame is the one who supplied the sleeping pill for you."

"Oh."

"Why did you ask that?" I distinctly heard lofty censure in his voice. "You think they figure anything that happens to a black person, it's gotta be his own fault? Some flour-faced Nazis just tried to kill you. Why are you worried about how it looks to some white people? Think you're letting the race down?"

Oooh. Touched a nerve there. Big-time.

She's a middle-class hypocrite playing the bohemian. Was that what he was thinking? What did we have here? A truly enlightened brother? Or was he mixing me up with himself? Was he talking about his own fears? Or had he really zeroed in on mine?

I decided discretion was the better part of etcetera and—for once—held my tongue.

"All right," I said. "You nailed me trying to be exemplary. I've been chastened, and you paid me back for what I said about you, okay? But it's a little more complicated than that. The management here is just not having the best luck with the coloreds from Elmhurst, Queens, lately."

He looked at me questioningly but didn't press for any explanations.

The silence fell again. "How about handing me that mirror?" I finally asked.

He plucked my makeup mirror from the bureau top and gave it to me. He stood at the foot of the bed quietly examining me while I examined my face. He was right: nothing broken. The bridge of my nose was a bit tender and there was a little lump on the back of my head. That was all. I didn't look half as bad as I imagined. In fact, the tonic effect of a good night's sleep seemed to be right there on my face. Satisfied, I nodded and handed the mirror back.

"Think you're going to be okay now?" he asked.

"Fine."

"Good. I just didn't want to leave you until I was sure."

"Listen," I called out to him as he prepared to leave, "you *do* have a place to stay, right? I mean, you really are living—uh—somewhere?"

"Yes. I don't need any help."

"Right, right," I said. "I kind of forgot for a minute there. I'm the one who needs all the help." *You're Mr. Perfect, aren't you, you prick?* Damn, was there nothing I could do right with this guy? He just kept outclassing me. He was a living reminder of my incompetence. Bet if he was looking for his aunt Vivian she'd be cleaned up and firmly in hand by now, her ass in a seat on TWA.

"What's your name?" he asked mildly.

I began to laugh then. That's right. We hadn't been introduced, had we?

"Nan."

"My name's Andre."

"Okay. Thanks again, Andre. I owe you one."

"You really do speak French very well," he said.

"I've got an idea, Andre. Why don't you start polishing your French, like you said yesterday. Why don't you pick up the phone there and order two breakfast trays with extra coffee."

I got one thing right, at last. Cheerful little Marise, the maid, was sick that day. Her replacement was indeed called Josette. She had never served me before, so she didn't even raise an eyebrow at finding two of us in the room.

I carefully moved his violin case aside and opened the shutters wide to let in the morning air.

"Keep polishing, Andre. Speak to me in French," I said, pouring more coffee.

"I don't know if I can hold up my end all in French," he said.

"That's okay. Do the best you can." I then began to speak in my senior-year seminar French accent, enunciating clearly but keeping my vocabulary colloquial, everyday: "First off, tell me what you're doing over here, if it's any of my business. Are you in school?"

"No. I got a little bit of money after my mother died—insurance—and I just headed straight over here. I'm planning to be . . ."

"Be what?" I asked when he hesitated.

"Famous maybe."

I cracked up.

"Well, you sure can play that violin. Is that what's going to make you famous?"

"Yeah. Yes and no. I want to do something with the music, sure. But I'm also taking notes for this book I'm thinking about writing."

"No kidding? What kind of book?"

"About black people in Paris. Musicians mostly, but others, too—dancers, soldiers, poets, whoever I come across. And not just the big ones like Josephine Baker and Wright and them. I mean people who worked to get over here and would do anything to stay. They were excited—proud to be here. Not like tourists, you know? Like there was something really at stake for them. People like me." He paused there. "And you."

I couldn't help it. I was fucking happy he had included me.

"I want to walk around in their footsteps," he continued, "look up their friends and families, if they had any, visit the places where they lived. Give them their due. It's hard to do something like that—start over in a strange place. Hard. Lonely. Scary. There's more than one way to be a black hero—to me, anyway. I want to tell people how admirable some of those folks were."

"*Formidable*," I said. "So there is a little of the race man in you after all."

His face went scarlet around the edges. But, thankfully, he laughed rather than bristled.

"Where'd you study music?" I asked.

"I went to Curtis."

"You're from Philadelphia?"

"No. Detroit, originally." There was a sourish expression on his face.

"Sounds like you didn't like it much."

He shrugged. "Wasn't just Detroit. I didn't like anything that much in the States."

"I can hear that," I said.

I wanted to say something more than that, but I couldn't quite form the words yet. The permutations of our relationship to the whole of America were endless. You could hate white people but not hate America. You could come to terms with the racism but never accept the insipid culture. You could view our disenfranchisement as a kind of massive swindle—all that blood, sorrow, loyalty, hope, and patience deposited over the centuries, and the check keeps bouncing. You could simply self-destruct. Like I said, endless. I figured I'd hear the particulars of his take on the thing soon enough.

"Like Baldwin said, 'I had to get out before I killed somebody.' Is that how you felt?"

"Something like that," he said, not looking at me. "More than likely, if anybody was gonna end up dead, it would have been me. Like I told you before, I'm hardly anybody's idea of fierce. Keep in mind that when I was little, I used to have to walk home carrying a violin. *And* these thick glasses. It was like wearing a sign that said *kick the shit out of me*."

"Kids are real nice to each other, aren't they?" I said, angry, but not just on his behalf. I was thinking about my friend Aubrey's treatment at the hands of some of our peers. "Who was it that saw your musical stuff and put you in school?"

"My mother. She could talk you out of your teeth. Got me scholarships to everything. We didn't have much. My father died when I was seven."

"What was she like, your mother?"

"White. Which made things even more interesting than they might have been."

Yeah, I thought as much. Aggressive as our DNA is, there were still little hints of the other in his face. "Tell me more," I said.

I divided the last of the coffee between our two cups. Boy! did I want a cigarette.

"Well, like they say, nothing lasts forever," he said. "You get over yourself, one way or another. I stopped running from fights. And the fellas stopped wanting to fight me around the time we all discovered sex. See, the girls liked me."

I grinned. "Yaaay, Andre! So you went from being the four-eyed sissy to the neighborhood chick magnet."

"You got it. For however brief a time, I was a hero."

"Fierce at last!" I raised the fist to him.

"No, I told you, I'm not. But I'll tell you who was. My mom. I don't know how she did it, exactly, but she's the one who—" He stopped there and didn't talk again until he had drained his cup.

When he spoke again, his voice had become thick. "A lot of things make me want to kill. And a lot of things I just don't care about anymore. All I care about now is becoming excellent at my work and being legit over here. Getting my papers, steady gigs, an apartment, whatever. 'Cause I am *not* going back. By the way, that was a load of crap I gave you about being a legal resident and having a permit, just in case you didn't already know.

"About the only thing that makes me want to fight now is other people telling me who I am and what I ought to be doing and who I ought to be doing it with."

"You mean you don't like having your blackness challenged?"

"My blackness is not open to challenge. My father was black, so that means I'm black. Period. I guess what I mean is, my people deserve to be honored by me, and I'm serious about doing that—but I deserve some honor, too, right? Who doesn't?"

"Yeah," I said. "Who doesn't? Are you all on your own now? No family?"

"No."

"How long have you been in Paris?"

"Five months."

"Made any friends yet?"

He shook his head. "Not really. Just some guys I met playing around town. The place I'm staying at belongs to one of my profs, but he isn't there now. He's been incredibly nice to me."

"What are you—"

He cut me off. "Just a minute! Hold up! Question after question after question. We're only talking about me. I want to know something about you and your stuff."

"You will, you will," I said. "Tell you what. Wait for me in the café downstairs while I get ready."

"Ready for what?"

"We're going to get seriously drunk."

"Are you joking?"

"Seriously, intentionally drunk."

"It's only ten-thirty," he said giddily. "In the morning."

"I know. But I'm about to tell you my life story, right? That's not something you do sober, my brother. And you've got to show me your Paris before I show you mine."

He picked up his violin and practically danced over to the door.

"It's good to be an international nigger, don't you find, Nan?"

"Yes, *mon frère.* It is kind of da bomb."

INSTEAD OF WAITING DOWNSTAIRS, he had run home to drop off his violin.

By late afternoon, we'd been walking and talking and drinking for hours.

I didn't figure on another excursion to the Right Bank so soon. But that was okay. Andre and I were wending our way all over the 8th while his nonstop Negro-in-Paris history rap unreeled like a guided tour cassette. The kid was amazing.

He had just given me the complete history of the concert hall called the Salle Pleyel, on the rue du Faubourg Saint-Honoré, where every famous brown person who had ever set foot in Paris—from the players in the old La Revue Nègre to W. E. B. DuBois to Herbie Hancock to Howlin' Wolf—had drawn an audience.

We stopped briefly for another drink, exchanged more life story tidbits, and pressed on.

It was Andre who pointed out the American embassy building to me, near the Place de la Concorde. But more important to him was the spot a couple of buildings away where once had stood the deluxe club Les Ambassadeurs. I heard all about Florence Mills's success there in 1926 and how Richard Wright had brought Katherine Dunham's dance troupe there to perform in the forties.

As we swept up the Champs-Élysées, he listed what Chester Himes and his wife had had for lunch at Fouquet's in 1959. All right, all right—slight exaggeration.

Sidney Bechet this, Henry Tanner that, Kenny Clarke this, Cyrus Colter that . . . Was I aware that *Art Blakey aux Champs-Élysées* was the only live jazz record that . . . Did I want to visit the site of Chez Josephine, la Baker's nightclub, before or after we saw the cabaret where Satie, Milhaud, *and* Ravel used to hang with her . . . In 1961, you know, both Bud and Dexter backed up Carmen McRae at the Paris Blue Note, but it wasn't called that anymore . . .

Who had told this child he wasn't black enough? Not to

play amateur Freudian, but his encyclopedic knowledge of our people in Paris was way past the maybe-I'll-write-a-book stage. It was obviously at the level of obsession. Who was he trying to vindicate?

It was late and I was starving. "I'm buying," I told Andre. "What do you suggest?"

"You shouldn't treat," he said. "You've been buying all day."

"It's okay. I'll write it off on my taxes under Educational Expenses."

"You know, there is a place I want to try."

"Name it."

"Bricktop's. It's in the ninth."

He was putting me on. "Oh sure," I said, laughing. "Maybe we'll run into Mabel Mercer and her friend Cole Porter. Scott and Zelda, too." Bricktop—the oh-so-sophisticated cabaret singer— and the club bearing her name were roaring twenties legends, I knew. He had to be putting me on.

"No, no. It's there. Really."

"You're really over the edge, man. I understood that Bricktop's closed about sixty years ago."

He grinned mischievously at me. "Yes, you're right. It did. But there's a place with the same name now. I'd like to see what it's like."

"That's better," I said. "I guess we won't have to get the net for you after all. Are we dressed for it?"

"I think we're cool. It's just a place with down-home food and a piano player."

BACK TO FUNKY PIGALLE. I had crisscrossed most of these streets before, in my scattershot search for Vivian. Well, this time I wasn't sitting around in the lobbies of grunge hotels, search-

ing for down-and-out bars or the Parisian equivalent to a soup
kitchen. I was being escorted around the hallowed grounds of
our ancestors, so to speak. The hotel where Bud Powell lived.
The cabaret (at least the address where once there had been a
cabaret) where one celebrated musician reportedly shot another
to death. And, of course, the site of the original Bricktop's on the
rue Fontaine.

I felt a flash of guilt about having taken the day off like this.
That would be old Ernestine trying to shame me: Vivian's suf-
fering! she was reminding me. Vivian's lost—broke—Vivian's
dying! And here you are, drinking the day away *with some man*,
chasing after some phantom of the glamorous black past.

Yes, ma'am, I answered meekly. I *am* having too much fun and
he *is* too good-looking. Tomorrow I widen the search for Aunt
Viv. I swear.

Cole Porter and Mabel Mercer were definitely not in resi-
dence. No ladies in backless evening gowns and diamonds. Not
a tuxedo in sight. The new Bricktop's was African American
kitsch. Autographed photos of the namesake lady herself, of
Louis Armstrong and Lady Day, Alberta Hunter and you name
them. Stuffed Topsy dolls. Posters for Oscar Micheaux movies.
Laminated Bessie Smith records. Items on the menu named after
this or that famous personage. The food wasn't half bad, though.
We devoured hot cornbread and smothered chicken and collards
while we goofed on the place. The generic old black gentleman
at the baby grand played terrific stride.

They were doing a fairly brisk business in the place, too.
Mostly older black people occupied the tables, but quite a few
younger couples—black, white, black and white—were chow-
ing down as well. Some musician types were drinking and shooting the breeze with the bartender up front.

A loquacious elderly gentleman we took to be the owner,
because of the deference being paid him by what appeared to be

the regulars, was holding court at a large round table near the back. The drinks were flowing back there, and spirits were high. One woman at his table we recognized as an up-and-coming diva from the States—you know, in one meteoric arc she goes from the church choir in Stomach Ache, Mississippi, to rave reviews at the Met. When Andre kept glancing over there, I assumed it was Miss Thing that he was staring at.

But no, he said, he was looking at the old man. There was something about him—something vaguely familiar—that he couldn't quite put his finger on.

"He was probably Eubie Blake's butler or something—somebody only you would know."

He blushed. At least he had enough perspective to be embarrassed.

I called for the check.

What a day it had been. We began the long walk back to the 5th, still talking, confiding in each other the way you do in the early stages of a friendship. Occasionally I'd point out a café or a restaurant or a street corner where I'd dined with friends, met some fascinating someone, made a discovery of one sort or another.

Back at last at the hotel, we were reluctant to say good night. I invited Andre up for a glass of the brandy I'd been smart enough to purchase and lay away in the armoire.

We set our chairs in front of the open window and went on talking. It wasn't long before a weird kind of chill went up my back. I knew it wasn't from the night air. It was a bizarre sensation and I managed to push it away quickly enough, but I had become somewhat distracted.

"I think I got it!" Andre exclaimed, seemingly out of the blue.

It was as if his voice was coming at me from the bottom of a well. "What? What did you say?"

I had been staring, transfixed, over at the top of the bureau.

"You know that old man—the one who owns Bricktop's?"

"Yeah. What about him?"

"Didn't someone call him Mr. Melson—or Melons?"

"I may have heard somebody call him something like that. Why?"

"I think I know who he is."

"Who?"

"Morris Melon. That's it. He was a teacher. Anthropology, wasn't it? Or sociology. Yes, right. He wrote a book—one of those pioneering studies about the black community in Chicago. Or am I thinking of *Black Metropolis*? It was something like that, anyway. Damn, what was the name of that book? Or was it the study of the Gullah Islands? I should interview him sometime. Find out his story."

He went on chattering. I was only half listening. I got up and began to walk around the room slowly, a sense of fear rising steadily inside me.

Andre had pulled himself out of his trip down memory lane. "What's the matter, Nan? What are you doing?"

I began to open the bureau drawers then, checking, I'm not sure what for. I looked inside my sax case, and all seemed well there. I could find nothing missing. But I knew that someone had been looking through my things. I just knew it: earrings placed at the right-hand corner of the bureau instead of the left; a tube of hand lotion set on its side rather than on end; panty-hose rolled up with the toes outside rather than in. But things disturbed so minutely that it was possible I was imagining the changes. I told Andre what I was thinking. Moreover, I said, I think it might have something to do with my aunt.

"What do you mean? It was probably just the maid."

I shook my head. "No. No, something's . . . something's happening."

"Like what?"

I had to shrug my shoulders. I had no idea what I meant.

He smiled at me and got me settled down again, almost convinced me that it was my imagination. I sat back at the window with him and finished my drink, but that weird feeling never went completely away.

"I'd better go," Andre said a while later, his voice low. "You need to get to bed."

I nodded. "So do you, friend."

He nodded, too.

A darkness moved across his face then. I didn't understand it. We stood for a minute in the doorway, saying a final good night, and then he left.

Seconds later, there was a knock at the door. He had come back.

"Forget something?" I asked.

"No. Look—uh . . ."

I waited in silence. The darkening in his face was full-blown midnight by now. Something was very wrong.

He dropped the bomb then:

"You think I'm gay, don't you?"

"Of course not." Oh yes, I did.

I hadn't known it before, but of course I did. What else could it mean for a handsome young man to be staying *chez* "one of my profs."

"I'm not," he said. He reached for my wrist but at the last moment pulled back. "I'm not."

I caught my breath. I didn't speak. He was looking at me so intently that I lowered my gaze from his.

"I'll come over to have breakfast with you tomorrow—if that's okay," he said finally. "We have to do something about your aunt."

We have to do something?

I nodded. "See you in the morning."

Okay, so maybe he wasn't a closet case. But surely there was more to his life story than brilliantly gifted mixed-race kid fights his way out of the ghetto and becomes the toast of Gay Paree. It wasn't that I suspected what he had told me was untrue; there simply had to be some juicy bits that he'd left out.

We.

When he was gone, I locked the door and placed my grip in front of it. Just in case I had not imagined the rearrangement of things in the room.

CHAPTER 4

IT COULD HAPPEN TO YOU

I WAS SHOWERED and in street clothes when he arrived.

He was carrying a white box tied with string.

"Coffee's on the way up," I said. "What's that?"

"Decent croissants," he answered, "and sliced ham and some fresh fruit. I stopped at the market near my place." He lifted the sack in his other hand. "And the morning paper."

He laid out all the items on the bureau. "This is the kind of stuff even I can afford," he said.

"Don't worry, boyfriend," I said. "You're going to be rich and famous soon enough."

Thank God, last night's heaviness seemed to have gone from his face, and from the air between us. The tray was delivered a minute later. He sat next to me on the bed and we breakfasted royally.

I felt good, happy, so much less alone.

Unfortunately, when I looked down at the headline under the

fold of the morning paper, that warm and fuzzy feeling instantly
went away.

AMERICAN WOMAN BRUTALLY MURDERED

My heart stopped beating for a moment.

Andre noticed the headline a second after I did. We began to
read frantically, looking for the name of the victim.

Polk. Mary Polk. A young white woman.

I could breathe again.

For about two horrible minutes, I had been absolutely convinced that it was Vivian who had been murdered. But now it
was just another story in the news. We read on.

The woman had been bludgeoned to death in the alleyway out
back of Le Domino, a seedy bar in Pigalle. She was apparently in
France on business, working for a wine wholesaler. She had been
registered at a perfectly respectable hotel in the 1st and was probably unaware that crime in the area had recently started to soar.

The article went on to say that another patron of the club,
one Guillaume Lacroix, had been detained for questioning but
already released. The police said Lacroix (street name Gigi) was
an ex-convict, a known thief and one-time pimp with a long
record, but there was no evidence linking him to the dead
woman. The continuation page of the story showed a mug shot
of Lacroix looking like a freeze-dried trout.

Another possible suspect, unnamed, was being sought. Authorities believed for now that robbery was the motive for the murder:
all Mary Polk's cash, jewelry, and credit cards were taken.

In the gruesome crime scene photo Mary Polk lay dead, a
bloody tarpaulin over her upper body, exposed from the knees
down. There was something lurid, and at the same time touching, about her shapely ankles in the high heels. Also pictured

was the murder weapon—a paperweight wrapped in a "blood-soaked kerchief, olive green in color and with a red insignia sewn on the upper-left corner," the news account said.

Sipping at my coffee, I put the paper aside for a minute. Andre picked it up and continued to read, narrating the rest of the story to me as he did so.

I was still thinking about my aunt Vivian. Vivian in her disco-going, coke-snorting, party-animal heyday. I had always admired the way she put herself together—stark black, tight-fitting dresses or bell-bottomed jumpsuits in startling colors. She would scour the flea markets for antique hats and jewelry and shoes. And she almost always wore a scarf. Not a flowing chiffon number, but something more like a cowboy bandanna—a kerchief. She said it added just the right element of fun to her outfits, kind of a throwaway. There was one sort she was especially fond of. A Girl Scout kerchief. Her waist was so tiny she could wear one of those as a sash. In fact, she collected them. She must have had a half dozen of those bandannas.

I took the newspaper from Andre's hands and stared hard at the bloody scarf wrapped around the lethal paperweight. Of course, it was impossible to make out any details in a photo like that, but—no. No, it was crazy. What I was thinking couldn't be true.

I jumped off the bed, startling Andre.

"Where are you going?"

"I must be the stupidest cow who ever lived," I said, jamming my feet into my boots.

"What are you talking about? Nan, where are you going?"

"Reception!" I shouted, fumbling with the door. "I'm going to get her suitcase! I should have looked in her suitcase!"

———————

HER VALISE WAS HUMONGOUS. I dragged it onto the birdcage elevator, off again, and into my room.

The case, an old one, was not locked. We hefted it onto the bed and unsnapped the fasteners. It had been packed tight as a drum. All manner of stuff sprang out and onto the coverlet— sweaters, trousers, pantyhose, shampoo—even a photo album.

"I wonder how long she intended to stay," said Andre. "There's a lot of crap in here."

"Yeah," I said, "you're right. And look at the kind of crap it is—I mean, the variety of crap."

There was an impressive panoply of stuff: hair curlers, an old matchbook from the Brasserie Lipp, a portable radio, light clothes, heavy clothes, a couple of mateless earrings, photographs, an empty perfume bottle. A lot of the things seemed more like mementos than travel necessities.

"You know what?" I said. "It's like she grabbed the minimum stuff a person would need to set up housekeeping. Almost like she was going to start a new life."

"She wasn't planning to go home, you mean."

"Maybe. The strangest thing of all is why she would leave it all behind."

"But you said she skipped on the bill."

"Yeah, I know. But if you're deliberately going to skip on the bill, wouldn't you find a way to take a few things out, you know, one at a time in a shopping bag on your way out one morning and nobody would think anything of it. If you were really planning to escape without paying the weekly rent, you'd smuggle your clothes out somehow and just leave the empty suitcase—or something.

"This makes it seem like she left here on the run. Like she hadn't planned to skip at all."

"Could be," he said, picking up the hefty photo album. "Do you remember this?"

"No. I hadn't seen her for a long time. I don't know what kind of things she would have kept at home—wherever that was."

We opened the cover of the album to the first page of photographs.

"That's my grandmother!"

In truth, I had never met my father's mother. She died young. But I recall this photograph of her; my father had a copy of it that used to adorn the chest of drawers in my parents' bedroom.

"God, how strange," I said. "It's so weird seeing that picture again after all these years."

Andre leafed slowly through the book. "He looks like you. Is that your father?" He was pointing to a tall, serious-looking young man in cap and gown.

"Yeah. He looks like he'd rather be someplace else, doesn't he? Like always."

"You don't get along with him?"

"I don't know if I'd put it that way. I don't see him often enough to get along or not get along with him. I was never really sure how Pop felt about me. I was grown up when he left, but it was almost as if when he stopped loving my mother, he stopped loving me, too."

"I don't believe it works like that," he said, lingering another minute before he turned the page. "Wow—is that *you*?"

"Where?"

The little girl in pigtails was wearing a polka-dot playsuit, grinning at the camera.

Lord, what a geek I was. I took control of the album and turned hurriedly past the next page or two lest we encounter any shots of me accepting spelling bee or good citizenship prizes.

"There's Vivian."

She was wearing a white suit and matching pumps, and a bridal veil. A black man I did not recognize was the groom.

"She's beautiful," Andre said. "Who's the man?"

"Uncle number one, I suppose. She's awful young there. I don't remember him."

"Look here," said Andre. "Looks like another wedding."

Yes, it did. I instantly recognized City Hall in Lower Manhattan. Viv, in a scalloped-neck sheath, her hair teased to giddy heights, and a devilishly handsome man—with an Afro as big as the Ritz—holding up a copy of their marriage license on the steps of the courthouse. Him, I had a vague memory of.

We continued to turn the pages.

Hubby #3 looked familiar, too. Jerry, that's what he was called. "The Cracker," I believe, was my father's pet name for him. Jerry was a musician from L.A. By the look of things, he and Viv had gone to Venice on their honeymoon. And here they were in swim clothes, on a hotel balcony, the Adriatic like a chip of sapphire behind them.

We saw Viv in one of those jumpsuits at a table in some bar. A second-level Motown crooner from the sixties was pawing her. Andre put a name to the guy's face: Chuck Wilson.

There she was again, in a colorful African head wrap, receiving an autograph from a nice-looking black man, the chairs and tables of a cabaret visible in the background. "That's Oscar Brown Jr.," Andre pronounced.

"You know, I think you're right," I said. "Who's this?" I pointed to the gentleman in another photo, seated at a Steinway, who was shaking hands with Vivian.

"I believe it's Wynton Kelly."

"You're kidding."

"No."

"And what about her?" I said, turning to a snap of Viv in her black evening finery, wineglass raised in salute to a sleepy-eyed lady, also at the piano of some boîte. I slipped the photo out of its cellophane jacket and turned it over, cupping it with my hand so that he could not see what was written there: "Shirley Horn at the Blue Note, 1971."

"Shirley Horn," said Andre.

"Boy, you are amazing. Who's this handsome guy—playing the bass?"

"Ray Brown."

Again, I took the snapshot out and looked at the back of it. He was right again. "Damn, you're good," I said.

He shrugged, trying to hide his swelling chest.

I took out another one and looked at it front and back. "I'm going to stump you on this one, I bet."

"Let's see it."

This time I handed the photograph to him. Vivian was pictured with a sweet-faced black man no taller than she was, but beautifully built. They stood with their arms around each other's waist under a sign that read in French EXOTIC GARDEN—THIS WAY.

He studied the man's face for a long time. "Well, I guess you got me," he admitted. "I can't identify him. Let's see who it is." He turned the photo over.

Picnic With Ez, near Èze! (Ha ha) was written on the back.

"What does it mean?" Andre asked. "Where is Èze?"

"On the Riviera. We'll have dinner and make a night of it in this incredible hotel someday. When we've got two thousand dollars to blow."

"You mean you've been there?"

"Uh-huh. Once."

"Who took you?"

I gave him a little world-weary sigh. "Oh, you know. Jekyll and Hyde. A mistake wearing pants."

That's the trouble with guys who know a lot more than you: they know *a lot* more than you. "I guess I come by my occasional bad taste in men honestly. God knows, Viv had her lapses."

He looked down at the snapshot again. "So maybe this guy Ez turned out to be one of her mistakes. But you say you don't know him?"

I shook my head. "Never heard of him."

We played the game for a few minutes more and then I dived back into the suitcase. More crap, as Andre had called it. But nothing to lead us any closer to Viv. No address books, no airline tickets, no names or phone numbers jotted down on paper napkins. And no Girl Scout bandannas. I guess Viv's waistline wasn't what it used to be.

Finally I came across a fraying denim jacket. I stood up and tried it on. A couple of sizes too small for me and my friends up top. I stuck my hand in one of the chest pockets and pulled out a filthy piece of paper, rolled up tightly like a reefer. I unrolled it. It was, to my astonishment, a hundred-dollar bill, US currency.

Andre and I began a thorough search, turning pockets inside out, feeling along seams, opening jars, and so on, but we could find no more cash.

"This was her emergency money, I guess," I said.

"Yeah," he said. "And from what you told me—her telegram to your mother and everything—she had a real emergency. Why didn't she spend it?"

It was a good question.

I put the money back and closed the case, sitting on the lid to get it refastened.

"Know what I think?" I said. "I think Viv left her room one day, just like always, and something happened to her on the outside. I don't know—she saw something or somebody who scared her or grabbed her or . . . whatever.

"Either that or she came back here to the hotel once and found somebody or something waiting for her, and she was too spooked to even come up and get her stuff."

I waited a few seconds, and when he didn't reply, I asked, "Doesn't that sound logical to you?"

This time it was Andre who made a sudden move. All at once he was clearing up the debris from our breakfast and opening the armoire where I kept my things and flinging open the drawers.

"What are you doing that for?"

"Get your stuff," he said. "We're getting out of here. You're leaving this hotel."

"And going where?"

"To my place."

"Why?"

He didn't answer.

"Why?" I asked again. "You think something's going to happen to me here. Is that what you're saying?"

"I don't know. But I think you should leave. You could save the money, in any case."

"You believe somebody was here last night now—is that it?"

"No—I mean, I don't know—it's possible. But aside from all that, I want you to come. I want you to stay with me."

I called downstairs and told them I would be checking out and that I'd need to retrieve the envelope I'd stashed in the safe.

"You know, Andre," I said when I had finished packing, "I bonded like this—with a strange man—once before. Only once."

"What happened?"

"Not good. Not good. It ended up terrible."

CHAPTER 5

STRAIGHT STREET

I SPRANG from the cab.

"Holy shit. You live on the rue Christine?!"

"Yeah," he said. "Didn't I mention it?"

"You most certainly did not, Andre."

"You're tripping because you know Baldwin once lived on this street. Is that it?"

"No, fool. I'm 'tripping' because I love this goddamn street like a schoolboy loves his cherry pie. When you said you got the ham in the market, you meant the market at rue de Buci, didn't you?"

He answered, but I wasn't even listening.

I was running up the stairs ahead of him.

"What floor?" I called down to him while he struggled with Viv's suitcase.

"Top."

Holy shit!

The tea shop across the street, with the madeleines to die for. The blind man in the fountain pen shop. The fifty-seat cinema at the end of the block. There was a time when I'd have crawled over broken glass to live on this block, sold my grandmother, given away my soul. I had been walking on the street perpendicular to this one, rue de Seine, one summer afternoon—I was nineteen years old—and I'd turned down this street and opened my arms to it. I couldn't even have told you why; there were far more beautiful places to live right in this neighborhood. But I had returned to this street again and again, walked it at all times of the day and night, observing the life that went on, pretending I lived in the apartment over the lingerie store. I used to see this street in my dreams after I'd returned to school that fall.

And now Andre was turning the key in the lock and letting me into—holy shit! A skylight. The apartment was tiny, but so beautiful. Was this really happening? I was flying around that room, touching everything—the lamp, the kitchen sink, the stereo.

I turned to face Andre, who was regarding me as if I were insane. I suddenly began to laugh helplessly. No wonder he thought I was nuts. I was acting like—like a schoolgirl version of Andre, when he had some Negro arcana in his teeth.

By the time my fit of laughter was over, his expression had changed. I knew that face: desire. Wrong word. Desire was the least of it. His face read, as clearly as the headline in the morning paper, You are going to be fucked. No preliminaries. No talk. For better or worse. Fucked.

I didn't contradict it, I didn't examine it. I was too busy tearing out of my dress.

I ran—ran—to my valise and tried to claw it open, looking for a condom. But he overpowered me, pinned me where I stood. I stopped struggling, fearing he would snap my windpipe with the strong hand at my neck. Fearing, period. I was afraid of him but even more afraid of the brute strength of my own desire as we fell to the rug with him tearing at my underpants.

He was on me. Everywhere. Prying me open. Sucking. Thrusting inside me like a wild boar. Crying out. With my nail, I had accidentally opened a small gash over his left eyebrow. We were either going to come together or kill each other.

There was unbearable grief in his throat when he finished. I dug my fingers into his hair, pulled his head up off my breast momentarily and looked into his eyes. His face was pasty and wet and he was sobbing. I covered his mouth with mine and we rolled over and lamely began to do it again.

Through his tears he spoke for the first time since we had entered the room. What he said was "Belong to me."

"I do," I said, not missing a beat.

HE MADE COFFEE with his back to me. Nothing on except his shorts. That wonderful barely there butt of his seemed to wink at me like a pornographic sign. A warming breath blew across my being, heating me up again. Inside my head, I went to the next time I would lie gasping under him, barely able to lift myself to him; the next time I'd lick at the sweat in the hollow of his neck in syncopation with the stroking of his finger. Greedy Nan, greedy girl. I pushed the image aside, busied myself with unpacking.

He got the windows open, then poured coffee and brought mine over to me in a small yellow cup.

"Nan?"

I looked up at him.

"I have never done anything like that before," he said. "Not even close."

"Neither have I," I said, "and I'm a slut. By some standards, I mean."

THE NEXT FORTY-EIGHT HOURS went by in a blur. I know I phoned Mom to tell her I'd—ahem—changed residences and to give her a no-progress progress report. I know Andre and I had two or three quick meals in the café across the street from the apartment. I know we made a couple of scouting excursions to low-down hotels and hostels to inquire about Vivian, and in desperation we did place an ad in the *Trib*. But mostly those two days, those hours, went by in a haze of the headiest, funkiest, sexiest sex I had ever taken part in.

The caveman-type coupling gradually faded into long looks and longer kisses and driving each other wild with touches and tongues, and doing it in the bathtub, and feeding each other cheese with our fingers, and generally going through each other like two kids with a box of cookies.

It was damn hard to keep my mind on Aunt Viv and her troubles. But on the third day, the fog began to lift, and I was able to focus a little better.

Andre and I went back to the hotel on rue du Cardinal-Lemoine that afternoon, just on the chance that Vivian had come back to pay her bill and collect her things. No such luck on that score. But the madame, to whom we presented a staggering bouquet of flowers, was good enough to conduct another phone search for us: this time to determine whether Vivian was in jail under any of her various names.

Andre and I were still unable to keep our hands off each other, but we had at least come back to earth sufficiently to be hungry for a homemade meal. On the way back to the apartment we stopped to acquire groceries and wine in the open-air market. I put the chicken in the small oven and set about peeling some potatoes. While I worked, he supplied a beautiful serenade—a medley of standards that sounded utterly fresh and even downright foreign on the violin.

After dinner the concert resumed. I was eating his "Don't

Worry 'Bout Me" with a spoon when he stopped mid-note, the queerest look on his face.

"What?" I said, pulling myself out of the reverie.

"I just got the greatest idea."

Wasn't it wonderful, my beloved had an idea.

"What idea?"

"You know 'Sentimental Mood,' don't you?"

"Sure," I said.

"Okay. And—let's see—what else? Do you know 'Blue Room'?"

"Of course."

"Go get your sax."

Duets!

Why the hell not? Talk about your peas in a pod. Two jazz-drunk African American neo-Francophiles.

I'd never given much thought to jazz violinists before I met Andre. Now I kicked myself for not making an effort to see artists like Regina Carter or Maxine Roach and the all-female group she was involved in back in New York: the Uptown String Quartet.

I was now of the opinion that violinists made the perfect musical colleagues. Stuff Smith had collaborated most successfully with Dizzy, and with Nat Cole and Ella. Who else? Joe Venuti, of course. Then there was the old gentleman they called "Fiddler"—Claude Williams, who, if he only had four arms, could accompany himself on the guitar. And, almost too obvious to mention: the Grappelli-Reinhardt combination.

The world thought I was just little old me from Queens. Ha! Little did they know, I was Django's illegitimate Gypsy granddaughter.

CHAPTER 6

LUSH LIFE

IT WAS TIME for a bold move.

Time was flying away from me. Before Vivian became nothing more than a memory, I had to do something forceful, something concrete. And I had to do it now.

That is why I made the decision to dip into the murky end of the pool, going once again to Pigalle.

As far as we knew, Vivian wasn't dead or dying. But that didn't mean she wasn't still in trouble. The way I saw it, if she was indigent, hungry, unable to go back to the hotel for her money, and surely unable to get any kind of job over here, she might well have turned to something not so legit, if not outright felonious. And so I decided to seek help from the only French criminal I knew—make that *knew of.*

The first bold step I took was to tell a whopping big lie to Andre. I said that I'd run into an old classmate in the drugstore. She was living in Paris and she and I were going to get together for a night of drinking, roasting men, and catching up. It was to be girls-only, I told him; next time we got together, I'd ask him to join us.

See, I knew he would go nuts if I told him what I was really planning to do. So he spent the evening playing with a couple of other musicians way out in Passy, while I joined my mythical girlfriend for dinner.

The newspaper accounts of the murder of Mary Polk, the American businesswoman, had made Le Domino, the club where she was killed, sound like sin central. But in fact it was sort of like the French version of the dive where my friend Aubrey danced in New York. A lot of drunks. A few ambulatory junkies. Watery booze and skinny sex workers and a bunch of randy men who ought to know better.

I chatted up the bartender and tipped outrageously and hung around long enough drinking donkey-piss beer to get my reward: Gigi Lacroix, the ex-pimp who had been questioned and released in the Mary Polk investigation, put in an appearance about 1 a.m.

Yeah, he was a bit oily. But I had been prepared for that. I didn't expect a guy in a beret carrying a marked-up copy of *Nausea* or humming Jacques Brel's greatest hits. I predicted a certain sleaze factor, and I got it. Gigi was a thin fellow with a thin mustache, a bad haircut, and a line of bullshit as long as a summer day in Stockholm.

The thing was, with his big Charles Aznavour eyes and Popeye swagger, he was kind of adorable along with it.

Gigi said he had not run a stable of ladies of the night in more than ten years; "that nonsense" was all in the past. To hear him tell it, he was an old coot now—enjoying his retirement and, for all he knew, "looking up the ass of death." Guillaume Lacroix claimed he was now just a regular *mec* who liked his dinner hot and on time, and of course a glass of wine now and then. *But . . .*

if a nice man was in dire need of female companionship, or if one person with something to sell needed an introduction to another person with the wish to buy? He broke off with that emblematic Gallic shrug. *"Entendu?"*

Understand? Sure I did, I said, managing to slide my hand out of his grip and signal the bartender for another round.

Unlike a lot of his stuffy countrymen, Gigi adored Americans, he assured me. Especially Al Pacino. Did I love the movies as much as he did?

Oh, absolutely.

Was I, or this fellow I was traveling with, involved in any way with the film industry?

Sadly, no, I had to admit, but we were both musicians—did that count for anything?

"Not really," said Gigi. "Paris is lousy with musicians—no offense." In any case, he said, he wasn't the one to talk music with. His lady friend Martine was the music expert. She'd probably be dropping in around two-thirty.

I saw no reason to fence with Gigi Lacroix. He was no more a cop lover than I was. I laid out the Aunt Viv story for him. Let's say it was the edited version of the Viv story. Leaving out any mention of the ten grand I was going to give her, I stressed how worried the family was about her; I was on a mission, out to rescue my adventurous aunt, who drank a little and who'd always had more nerve than brains.

While Gigi listened, he casually downed another in the army of Pernod I was paying for.

"Hmph," he uttered at the end of the tale. "I don't know the lady. She sounds like an exciting woman, though."

"Do you think you could help me? Do some asking around?"

There went another defining gesture: the puffed-out lips accompanied by raised eyebrows and a slant of the head. Maurice Chevalier in polyester. The guy cracked me up.

I figured we could come to terms.

"*Écoute*, Gigi," I said, "you're not going to be able to retire to the mountains on what I can pay you, but I think we can work something out. There's just one thing I've got to get straight."

"Of course," he said expansively.

"Did you have anything to do with Mary Polk's death?"

The false bonhomie fell away from his face then and he shook his head once. "The unfortunate victim," he said, "was another lady I never had the pleasure of meeting. We simply happened to be in the wrong place at the wrong time—both of us."

I had a sudden image of that Girl Scout bandanna. It just flew in and out of my thoughts. "Did you get a look at the death scene? Out back I mean, where the police found her?"

"Me? No, my friend. I'm no ghoul. I have no curiosity about the dead. Especially when the police are involved."

I took that in without comment.

So it was that I threw in with Gigi the aging pomaded pimp—with the promise that if he tried to fuck me over, he'd have to call in Al Pacino to get me off his case. I'd make his retirement uncomfortable as hell, even report to the police that he'd told me he knew who killed Mary Polk as well as my aunt.

Did he take my threats seriously? Not very, I wagered. But I decided to go with him anyway.

It was while he was comparing *Godfather III* to the other installments in the saga that Martine walked in. Gigi Lacroix was like a thousand other trifling guys I'd seen in the world: unregenerate larceny in his heart, living off the weaknesses of others, quick-witted, shrewd, and lazy. When all was said and done, a colorful underworld character, no more. His lady friend Martine, on the other hand, scared the bejesus out of me.

For starters, my girl had a *scar*—jawbone to neck. No taller or more powerfully built than he, but there was menace in her very walk. She locked glances with Gigi, ignoring me utterly until he introduced us, at which time she swept her burning eyes across my face and torso. I looked down at her stiletto-heeled shoes, which consisted entirely of straps and laces that crawled up her ankles like garter snakes.

Martine seemed to take up all the space at the bar. She and Gigi went into a wanton lovers' clutch for a couple of minutes and then he ran down my story for her. She reacted with nothing more than a snort, helping herself to a belt of Gigi's Pernod.

IT WAS AFTER 4 A.M. when I got back to the rue Christine apartment. Andre was sleeping peacefully, waking only long enough to ask if I'd had a good time with my fictitious chum—and he wasn't one of the guys we roasted, was he?

No way, I said, and pressed his head back onto the pillow. Then I went in to shower the stale tobacco and barroom fumes out of my pores.

When we got up the next morning, I'd have to tell him the truth about the evening and prepare him for Gigi.

AS PREDICTED, he was not amused. I saw the worst of his play-it-safe side as he turned into my father for fifteen minutes. He blasted me for my foolishness in going into that den of iniquity, preached at me for jeopardizing our status as nice colored foreigners, ridiculed my private-eye fantasies, and so on.

I sat there and took it. But, under my patient, reasoned, point-by-point defense, he had to agree in the end that playing it safe was getting us nowhere with the Vivian quest.

Once we had a late breakfast and hit the streets, he continued to punish me for a couple of hours with all the quickstep melodies he could think of. I was hungover, but I'd be damned if I wouldn't keep up with him.

The folks at the outdoor tables loved our ass. They were giving us an overwhelming round of applause. Andre's violin case was stuffed with francs. We had played duets all over Paris, and this was one of our favorite spots. We made just as much or more here as at Au Père Tranquille or the gargantuan café on rue Saint-Denis where the sex workers sometimes helped us with our pitch or playing for hours in the Métro.

"Could you *play* any faster?" I said through my teeth.

"Stop being sarcastic and concentrate," he said. I wanted to slap him.

Not really true. Number one: whenever I looked at that mouth of his, smirking, smiling, whatever, all I wanted to do was die in his arms. Number two: he had done the impossible—flogged me, metaphorically that is, until I learned to play Bird's "Segment" at the proper breakneck speed. How could I be mad at him? Andre believed I was a better musician than I did, and whether he was right or wrong, I had, beyond question, improved immensely. I could feel it happening, evolving, every day I spent with him. It was as if I were topping myself in a cutting contest with me.

"We're knocking off now—right?" I threatened, already packing up. Little or no sleep last night, I was exhausted.

"Yeah, right," he said. "Let's go home."

He put an arm around me and together we tripped across the avenue de la Grande Armée in the kind spring air. Through the traffic, across the noisy boulevards and the narrow streets we went, not talking at all. We were heading back to the apartment to clean ourselves up, and inevitably to make love, before going to meet Gigi for dinner. Life was so good it almost scared me.

Almost. There was no need yet to feel the gods were about to lower the boom on my perfect life. Because of course life wasn't perfect. I had not found Vivian. Indeed, I had not come within a mile of finding her—not a single lead—and it was starting to eat

me up inside. I'd be happy if Gigi turned up even the slightest
little piece of information.

Back in the safety of the little love nest on rue Christine, I
took a nice nap in the afterglow of afternoon sex. Odd how afternoon dreams are the worst, but afternoon sex is often the best.

Around seven that evening Andre and I pulled into virtually
matching outfits: black jeans and white shirts. Each checking the
other out and gaining assurance that we looked really cool, we
left the apartment and caught the Métro at Saint-Michel, heading for the bistro in the Bastille where Gigi liked to eat.

The place sure had the right smell. Onion and rosemary, rabbit and scallops, sweetbreads and hundred-year-old cheese and
rich red wine danced around my senses. I searched the noisy,
plain room for Gigi, but he had not yet arrived. We took a table,
the burner under my appetite suddenly cranked up to red alert.
Andre and I were devouring olives when I caught sight of Monsieur Lacroix, the lovely Mam'selle Martine in tow.

We had a sensational meal. And I bet there wasn't another
foursome like us in the place: Gigi and I doing most of the talking as he reported on the people he'd asked about Aunt Vivian;
Andre looking a little uncomfortable but gamely trying out his
newly mastered French idioms on Gigi; and Martine, who clearly
thought Gigi's mission was preposterous, barely speaking at all
but commanding and drinking wine as though—well, as though
she was paying for it.

"We are fairly sure your aunt is not in the life," Gigi pronounced.

Well, that was nice to hear. Aunt Viv, as far as Gigi could
determine, was not currently a prostitute. I stole a quick glance
at Martine, who was guffawing.

Martine seemed as eager to show off her rather good English as
Andre was to master colloquial French. "So what is this story?"
she said expansively, helping herself to more wine, "the two of

you are playing what? That . . . *jazz?*" She formed the word as if it were some mildewed thing she had come upon in the refrigerator.

"That's right," I said. "What's the matter? Don't you like jazz?"

She shrugged. "It is useless. Anyone can play popular music."

"Oh really?" I said mildly. "What sort of music do you admire, Martine?"

"Ze blues," she answered immediately.

Andre and I exchanged looks. I had to admit, his was more amused than mine.

"People are always speaking about these jazz men," Martine said dismissively. "How brilliant they are, how sophisticated. I say 'shit' to sophistication. The only real American music is the blues. Can you and your man with his silly little girl's pigtails do what John Lee Hooker does? (*Jean Lee Ook-heir.*) Do you have his pain? Do you have his *cri de coeur*? Or Lightning Hopkins (*Op-keens*)? No! You can play your childish ballads all you want, but you will never make anyone feel the way Muddy Waters did. No. You *have* no feeling compared to them. No soul. I do not care how black you are."

What could I do? If I got up and bitch-slapped her, which was what she deserved, it was going to cause no end of trouble. Gigi might pull out of the deal and leave me right back where I started. Or, just as likely, Martine, despite the thirty pounds I had on her, might end up kicking the shit out of me. I kept my seat. It had to be the high road for now.

"Well, thank you, Martine," I said crisply. "That was most informative. Tell me, is Muddy Waters your very favorite noble savage?"

"Do not patronize me."

"Patronize *you?*" That was Andre, not so amused anymore.

She shirked off his remark. "If you are really interested in who I like—for me, there is no one like Haskins. He was the best blues man of them all."

Haskins? Who the hell was that?

I looked to Andre, Mr. Information, for help. But apparently he, too, was drawing a blank on the name.

"It does not surprise me that you have not heard of him," Martine said sniffily. "See, Mr. Pigtails? I told you, you know nothing about the soul."

The three of us—Gigi, the slow-boiling Andre, and I—all sat back as Martine launched into her lecture.

"Little Rube Haskins," she said, "was a giant. A hero. He was unfairly locked up in your racist Mississippi prisons. But he escaped, first to Canada and then to Marseilles. Finally he came to Paris. He was the last in a line of giants like Leadbelly and 'Owling Wolf."

Andre listened intently as she rattled on. "Are you telling me," he said when at last she stopped for a breather, "this Haskins was living and singing in Paris in the 1970s?"

"Yes, that is right."

"And he wrote all these songs himself, you say?"

"That is right."

"But . . . but how come I don't know anything about this genius? I mean, why doesn't his name turn up in anybody's book? Why don't we see him listed as the composer on any folk music? How come I never once even heard the guy's name?"

Martine used Gigi's disposable lighter to fire up her cigarette. She took a luxurious puff from it and then said, "You expect me to explain your ignorance to you? This I cannot do."

Sharp intake of breath. Like he was counting to ten. "I don't suppose you have any of his records?"

"Records!" Martine scoffed. "Records? He had no records. The music industry is interested only in money, not in the truth. Haskins was appreciated only by the aficionados. Besides, just as he was about to go into the studio to make an album—he died."

"So how did you hear him? You went to these places where the aficionados hung out? Or to some kind of underground concerts?"

"What are you talking about, you ignorant man? I never saw him in my life. How old do you think I am? I was only a girl then. I've heard the tape recordings made of him at the clubs. They're collector's items today."

Andre gave her a lingering look of appraisal, full of skepticism.

Gigi, draining his glass, placed a proprietary arm around Martine's shoulder. "My Martine is like an encyclopedia, you know. Full of information—and opinions—no?"

"Yeah," said Andre, in English. "Full of it."

I gave him a sharp look.

"Hey, Martine," he challenged, "what's your favorite song by this giant—what's-his-name—Rube Haskins?"

" 'The Field Hand's Prayer,' " she snapped right back at him.

"The what?" He reared back in his chair, openly laughing at her.

This time, the look I threw him had broken glass in it.

"You find it funny?" Martine said, going red at the ears. "You think Haskins could not write a song better than the weak, pitiful white immigrants you jazz musicians worship? You would rather hear something by Cole Porter than the words coming from the heart of the descendant of a slave? What sort of idiot does this make you?"

Oh shit.

To quote my friend Aubrey, *What you have to say that for?*

Andre's eyeballs were orbiting their sockets. Spittle at the corner of his mouth. Fists clenched. All the signs of a man about to go ballistic.

He leaned toward her threateningly. "Listen, you skank, what you know about the blues—" was all I let him get out before I smashed into his ankle with my low-cut boot.

"Andre!" I called into his face like a drill sergeant. "We'll have Martine over for a night of shop talk some other time! We've got plenty of other stuff to talk about right now, don't we, Andre?"

He was fuming, but he shut up and, except for the stray wise-crack, remained that way while I passed a few more hundred francs to Gigi and listened to his rundown of where he was going to go later that night to ask about Vivian's whereabouts. I wrote down the phone number at the rue Christine apartment and he tucked it into his pocket.

Before the party broke up, Martine had an Armagnac and ordered espressos for all. Generous of the cow, wasn't it? I didn't want any goddamn coffee, but she had moved too quickly. I paid the check, glowering at her and at Andre.

We parted from them on the street, Gigi bursting with good manners and goodwill.

"Stop worrying," he said reassuringly. "I will find your way-ward aunt."

"Y'all can stop worrying, too," Andre muttered under his breath. "Why don't you take a fucking cab to the Delta—on us. Check out some authentic blues."

I waited until our dinner companions turned the corner before loosing my rage on my lover.

"Starting a fight over some lame-ass singer with that dumb bitch. What is the matter with you?"

"What do you mean, *starting*? I didn't start it! That dumb bitch had the nerve to talk to me about slaves!"

"Shut up! You let that silly woman bait you. You let your know-it-all musical ego run away with you—like it was your balls on the line instead of finding Vivian. Finding Vivian! That's the real point here, remember? I wouldn't give a rat's ass for Martine's musical opinions, either, but I can't afford to let this guy Gigi go yet. It'd be like flushing my money down the toilet, and we still wouldn't know anything. It's . . . It's . . . Dammit, what is the matter with you, Andre!"

Our second public brawl. Screaming at each other—that's how this relationship had started. We went at it full throttle there in front of the restaurant, a few curious onlookers, non–English speakers, I guessed, treating it as though we were the evening's entertainment: like we were street theater.

We used the walk home to cool down.

BY THE TIME we shut the door of the apartment behind us, I was exhausted all over again. I put on water for herbal tea and grudgingly made enough for Andre as well.

I plopped his cup down in front of him at the table.

"I'm sorry," he mumbled.

I grunted.

"I'm *really* sorry."

That sent me into his lap.

"I'm trying to do what's right, Andre," I said. "I'm just trying to do right by Auntie Viv. I don't know, maybe I'm feeling guilty because I used to wish Viv was my mother instead of—instead of my perfectly serviceable lovely mom. Pop treated Viv so bad, you know? Just because she decided she wasn't going to be a housewife in Queens—just because she wasn't all buttoned up and appropriate like him. Because she wanted to be free. I loved her for showing me that. I fucking *owe* her for that. Viv made a lot of stupid moves, but she lived her life—you know? I have to find her, Andre. Not just because of the money—I want to know she's okay."

"I understand," he said, rocking me a little.

"I was awful to you, wasn't I?" I said. "Cussing and carrying on like that."

"Yeah, you were an awful bitch. A real *margère*—a shrew."

"*Mégère*," I corrected him.

"Thank you, teacher. Let's go to bed, let's go to bed, let's go to bed."

I laughed. "So a crying woman gets you hard, huh?"

"A paper clip gets me hard, Nan. I want you right this minute."

No time to undress. Push the hot tea aside. Straddling him on the little wooden chair. He unbuttons my jeans. Shirt over my face. My arms immobile. Can't see him, what he's doing. Just feel him, working his way in. Poking blindly at his eyes. Fight free of the shirt, buttons popping. Tugging on his braids. He's picking me up. I'm gummy with lust. Irradiated.—"I'm sorry."— "I know."—"I love you."—"I know."—"Don't leave me."— "I won't. Promise to play the Ravel for me, after," I say through a giggle.—"Yes. All right. Oh yes," he says.

PRESSED TIGHTLY up against my back, he soaped my hair.

"I've got a surprise in store for you," said Andre, straining to be heard over the knocking of the old pipes in the shower stall.

"Ha! That ain't no surprise, Geechee. You get one of those just about every half hour."

"No, not that," he said. "This is something we have to go outside for."

"What? Where?"

"It's on the street."

"What street?"

"I don't know the name of it. We just have to walk till we find it."

"It" turned out to be a dusty, narrow shop near the Comédie-Française. It specialized in music scores and art relating to music. The two older women who ran the place nodded warmly—maybe even conspiratorially—to Andre and let us wander undisturbed all over the shop. I was in hog heaven, oohing and aahing over a photo of Billy Strayhorn arm in arm with Lena Horne, when Andre disappeared up the aisle. I could hear him exchanging hushed words with one of the ladies. In a minute the two of them approached me carrying a framed pen-and-ink sketch.

Andre turned it so that I could see it full view.

"Monk!" I screamed.

"*C'est beau, oui?*" the owner said, smiling.

"It's beautiful," I agreed.

"And it's yours," said Andre.

"Mine?" I grabbed it out of his hands. "Really *mines?*"

"Yeah, I bought it—in three installments."

I gave him a dozen kisses.

We were having a great time in there. While the sketch was being wrapped, I continued to browse. I went up and down the rows, flipping through all kinds of memorabilia and photos. It was in the bargain rack marked "Miscellaneous" that I came across the most startling piece of all.

"Andre!" I shouted out.

They must have thought I'd been bitten by a fat sewer rat or something, because all hands rushed over to where I stood.

"What is it?"

"Look at this photograph!" I pointed to a shiny headshot of a pomaded black man trying to look pensive and irresistible. "Look at the caption and tell me if I'm dreaming."

"Jesus Christ," Andre said. Just that.

"*Little Rube Haskins,*" I quoted the caption. "It says this is Martine's hero, Rube Haskins—right?"

"Yeah. It does."

"Man, do you know who this *is?*" I said, my eyes popping. "Take a good look."

"I don't have to," he replied. "That's your aunt Vivian's friend. Ez—from Èze."

CHAPTER 7

POP!POP!POP!POP!

NOT THAT WE HAD anything much to celebrate, but Andre and I went clubbing that night. Bricktop's.

The joint was jumping.

I had bought that amateur photo of Rube Haskins and we had run home from the music shop to compare it with the one in Vivian's scrapbook. No question about it; my aunt's Riviera companion and the obscure blues genius called Rube Haskins were one and the same man.

Sitting in the apartment, looking in bewilderment from one picture to the other, I got one of those *wow! why didn't I think of it before?* flashes. The original Bricktop had been a social lion. Everybody who was anybody in jazz-age Paris had passed through her door. Perhaps it was the same kind of thing with the present owner of Bricktop's. He might actually have known Haskins.

"Let's get over there," I urged Andre. We could talk to the owner before we hit the streets to play tonight.

It was one move that Andre had no trouble endorsing. It seemed safe enough to go and talk to Morris Melon. He was no ex-pimp with a razor-scarred girlfriend, and it seemed unlikely he'd make us pay by the hour for a little conversation.

I wriggled into my long, tight brown skirt with a matching sweater cropped so short that its hem fell just below my nipples. I tucked the Rube Haskins head shot into my purse and Andre and I grabbed our respective axes and headed out into the night.

Like I said, the joint was jumping. In fact, the whole town was bustling. After all, it was springtime in Paris. Folks at Brick-top's were finger popping and flirting, eating and drinking with abandon, and gathering around the pianist to request their favorite songs.

The elderly proprietor was just as much in the spirit as his customers. Morris Melon was drunk as a lord.

Leaning on his spiffy cane, he was up near the entrance greeting people as they walked in.

Small man, big voice. "Children!" his basso rang out when we stepped across the threshold. "*Bienvenu!*"

"*Merci*, Monsieur Melon," I said as he waved us to the crowded bar. "Will you allow us to buy you a drink?"

"Lord yes," he agreed, and joined us there.

Andre started out slowly enough but was soon in high gear with his music and tell-me-about-being-black-in-Paris quiz. We listened attentively while the old man pontificated and reminisced and testified, though I suspect that Andre already knew the answers to most of the questions he posed.

After he had related yet another fascinating anecdote about his life in Paris—and to be fair, his stories *were* fascinating—we zeroed in on the real target.

"Mr. Melon," I said, "we have a French friend who's wild about a blues singer who used to live in Paris. I'd like to get her some of his records, but I can't find any of them for love nor money. Do you know anything about him? Little Rube Haskins was his name."

He burst into high-pitched, derisive laughter. "'Rube' is right, *ma chère*. He was right off the boat. What the children in Chicago used to call a country nigger. To paraphrase that Ozark woman's song—a little bit country, a little bit rhythm and blues."

"You mean you actually met him?"

"Once or twice. You know what they say—if you stay in Paris long enough, you meet everyone in the world."

"Did you ever hear him perform?" asked Andre.

Melon rolled his eyes.

"No good?"

"Good and bad didn't come into it. He was ridiculous. He could play that guitar well enough, I'll give him that, but his songs about his mule jumping over the moon or some such were so derivative and falsely primitive as to be preposterous. None of the sweetness, none of the heart, the grace of the rural Negro—no blessedness. And I should know, child. I'm a proud country nigger myself. I just found the man vulgar, to be candid. But then again . . . oh, I don't know why I'm fussing so much. I suppose he was just trying to enjoy the party, like the rest of us. Let's just call him a footnote to a footnote, at best. I can't imagine that anyone let him make any recordings."

"When did you know him?" I asked. "How long ago?"

"Ah. Well, I'm not sure. Who's to say? The way time collapses on itself when you get to be my age. Time doesn't mean a great deal to someone like me, you know. Not anymore." He laughed that marvelous deep laugh again and took the fresh martini the barman handed him.

"Might I just show you something?" I said.

"Of course. Show me everything, dear girl."

I retrieved the glossy photograph from my bag and held it close to his hand resting on the bar.

"Is that what he looked like?" I said.

"Have mercy!" He stared at the photo for a long time. "Yes, I do believe that's him. Don't tell me your friend carries his picture around?"

"Well," I said, "she does adore him. She found this shot of him in one of the stalls on the Seine."

He turned the photo over in his hands a couple of times. "The French are peculiar, *n'est-ce pas?*" he said philosophically. "Wonderful—but peculiar. And would we have it any other way?"

After a moment's appreciative laughter, Andre asked, "What happened to Haskins, Mr. Melon? We heard he died young."

"Umm. I think that's true. Died young and died tawdry, if I'm remembering it right. Let me see—must have been a drunken brawl somewhere—no—it was a jealous husband—or a woman scorned—something like that. He was shot to death in a car was the story. Something like that. He didn't have the decency to just choke on a pig's foot."

I couldn't help it: I let out a shriek of laughter.

"Oh, I'm mean, child," Mr. Melon said. "I'm just terrible, ain't I?"

Melon slid smoothly from his barstool, cane and all, when a party of five came barreling in, shouting their greetings at him.

I had to get in just two more quick questions before he took his leave of us.

"By the way," I said, "did you happen to know any of Rube's lady friends? One in particular called Vivian?"

"Oh dear, I don't think so." He pursed his lips then. "The only Vivian I recall from those days was a young man, not a young lady. A British chap, and the less said about him the better."

"Last question," I said. "Any idea if Rube Haskins was his real name? I mean, did you ever hear people call him by any other name?"

He shook his head "Just 'fool.'"

"Well, thanks anyway," I said.

"You children should have some of that beautiful red before you leave tonight. It's delicious. Ask Edgar to pour you some."

"He's something, isn't he?" Andre said when Melon was out of earshot.

"He's a stitch. But I wouldn't want him to read me. He's got one sharp tongue."

"What now?"

"Yeah. You got that right. What now? We know for sure now this is Haskins. But where does that leave us? How did he go from Ez to Rube—or vice versa? And which one was he when Vivian went picnicking with him?"

Andre began to speak, but he stopped short when Morris Melon reappeared at the bar.

"Is it true what I hear, children?" he asked us excitedly.

We looked at him blankly.

"That's right, play it coy." He laughed expansively. "Don't be so modest! Some friends tell me you two are the talk of the town. They say *le tout Paris* is buzzing about the duets you've been performing. You must favor us with something."

His slow, steady clapping caught fire and before we knew it the whole restaurant was filled with coaxing applause.

After a brief consult with the pianist, we started with the old Nat Cole arrangement of "Just You, Just Me." A real up number. Everybody seemed to enjoy it. Then the old musician removed himself to a table and left us on our own.

Andre's beauty obbligato for me on "Something to Live For" seemed to come out of nowhere. Gorgeous. I was inspired and tried to return the favor for his solo work on "I Didn't Know

About You." Someday you've *got* to hear that on the violin. We closed with "I Didn't Know What Time It Was."

I guess we killed. Applause like thunder. The waiters began to anoint us with complimentary drinks.

Andre and I recaptured our places at the bar, and Morris Melon hurried over to clink his glass with mine. "You children are too beautiful to live," he cried in delight. "I want you to promise you'll come and play for us at least once a week."

Andre began to stutter and fumble for words.

"I won't take no for an answer," Melon pressed. "We'll feed you right, offer you our finest wines—I shouldn't overstate, decent wines, at least—and you can put your own tips bowl out on the piano."

Andre and I looked at each other and shrugged. We nodded okay at the old man.

"Babies," he said, grinning, "I couldn't be happier."

IF YOU DON'T KNOW what boulevard Saint-Germain looks like at four in the morning as you sit outdoors at Les Deux Magots . . . I won't spoil it for you by talking about it.

We had received all those strokes from the fabulous Morris Melon; the street crowds had been super generous; we'd stopped at one of my old haunts, an all-night place, for a perfect little meal; I was actually living on rue Christine, my street of dreams; the low sky was showing Paris pink around the edges; and, not least, this beautiful man I was in love with, was in love with me, apparently to the point of stupidity.

Again, heaven seemed almost within my grasp. But I couldn't be happy. I couldn't rest. We were no closer to finding Vivian. She was, if anything, slipping further away.

"You gotta do something for me tomorrow," I said, turning to Andre.

He polished off his almond croissant. "You mean today, don't you, sweetheart?"

"Right. Here's the thing: Vivian knew this guy Rube Haskins."

"Check."

"Only he had a different name."

"Check."

"And he was murdered—maybe over a woman, maybe *by* a woman."

"Check— Wait a minute. You don't think your aunt was the woman—or the woman scorned?"

"The pig's foot, so to speak. Of course I don't know that she had anything to do with it. But at any rate, it had to be in the papers, right? There has to be some kind of investigation when anybody gets murdered. And Haskins was a public figure, even if he was a really minor one—Mister Footnote. We have to find out if the police ever got the whole story. If they arrested anybody. Maybe somebody from his family came over here to claim the body. Maybe Vivian's name turns up as just someone the cops contacted for information."

"Maybe, maybe this, maybe that" he said. "So what is it you want me to do?"

"The murder happened, what, about twenty years ago. I'm going to make a run to the library tomorrow and make a phone call or two to some of the newspapers. I'll comb through the back issues. Not *Le Figaro*, it's too proper and conservative. But the tabloid types. That stuff's got to be on microfiche now, just like in the States. I'll try to find one of those books in English—you know, those music encyclopedias—*Who's Who in American Music*, or something like that—and see if Haskins's bio is there, and maybe his real name: Ezra Something, or Something Ezekiel—or whatever.

"What I need you to do is try to find back issues of the most obscure kind of music magazines you can think of. Canvass all your street player buddies and ask them if they own such things, or where to start looking. Maybe one of those music journals did a memorial piece on Haskins. Hell, maybe something a little more mainstream—like an early issue of *Rolling Stone.* Those shouldn't be too hard to find. Anything you can think of, no matter how nutty it seems. It's worth a try."

TRY WE DID. None of the arcane, or nutty, sources panned out. But, as I had speculated, there was mention of Little Rube Haskins's death in the police blotter sections of the conventional press. The only report of any length turned up as an ordinary news item in a Paris paper that had long ago ceased publishing. Minimal information emerged on Haskins—not even where he was born. He was referred to as a black American who resided at a modest hotel in the 11th arrondissement. In the last report on file (the story had run for two days) Inspector Pascal Simard declared that police were still looking for the vicious killer who had left Monsieur Haskins's mangled body in the one-way street where he resided.

I kind of enjoyed playing the puppet master, dispatching Andre to do this or that spadework. While he was following up one potential lead, I gigged on the street all by myself, which was kind of scary but thrilling. But then the rest of my afternoon was shot, as I had to go hunting for pantyhose long enough for my endless legs. I finally found my size at a little lingerie store where only nuns shopped.

Controlling my other operative, Gigi Lacroix, was a tad trickier. It was tough getting an appointment with him before sundown. He kept hours similar to my friend Aubrey's—the vampire schedule. Daylight must have been rough on his sensitive skin. He finally agreed to meet me at what he daintily referred to as teatime.

Gigi was waiting for me at a sedate "lady food" sort of café near the Louvre. The place was one of those unfortunate pissy hybrids of French and British culture where the waitress sneers at you if your shoes weren't made in Belgium. No trouble spotting Gigi among all the newly coiffed girlfriends in that joint. But at least the lovely Martine was not in attendance. That was a gift, and I was truly thankful for it.

"I have a little news for you," he said, using his napkin to wipe a spray of powdered sugar from his mustache. "Don't get your hopes up too high, though."

"What is it?"

"A friend who works the Eiffel Tower says he thinks he knows Tante Vivian."

"What!"

"Yes."

"What do you mean, he works the Eiffel Tower? What kind of work?"

"He's a pickpocket. I'm going to see him tomorrow. Chances are he's full of shit and just looking to make a few francs for nothing. But I'll give you a report."

"You won't have to. I'm coming with you."

"No, no, my friend."

"Yes, yes, my friend."

"I said no." Not a trace of his usual rueful charm in that. "It's no fucking place for you, where I'm meeting him. You'll only be in the way. Besides, you'll attract attention to yourself—and me. The last thing I need."

"Well, what about what I need, buster? What the hell kind of place is this where you're meeting?"

"No more questions. You're better off just letting me do what you asked me to do. Anything could happen—*entendu*? You're a Yank, remember. No matter how fancy your French accent is.

How would you like to end up deported? Who'll rescue your sweet old aunt then?"

"Why do you put it like that—my 'sweet old aunt'? What are you trying to say, Gigi?"

His laugh was almost as nasty as one of Martine's. "I'm not so sure. But my friend says if this aunt of yours is the same woman he's thinking of, she's up to her old tricks again."

"What does that mean?"

"Hey! Don't break my balls, *'pute*. Those are not my words. They're his. Like I said, he may just be giving me the runaround. I'll call you. Here . . . try one of these." He proffered his plate, which was crowded with cream-filled delicacies. "A girl with an ass like yours doesn't have to watch her weight. Am I right, *petite*?"

"Gigi," I said in exasperation, "get the fuck back into your coffin."

CHAPTER 8

MOUNTAIN GREENERY

THERE IT WAS. Etched in stone: LE PALAIS DU JUSTICE. The palace of justice, eh? I'd be the judge of that.

Actually, police headquarters, which is where I was headed, is next door to the *palais du justice.* The lettering on the police building didn't say a damn thing about justice.

If I'm not mistaken, a number of famous French people—real and fictional—have been associated with the Quai des Orfèvres. The quai was where Inspector Maigret was based, of course. At the urging of my high school French teacher I had read all those George Simenon novels about the eccentric detective. And quite near police headquarters, someone had told me, Simone Signoret and Yves Montand had for years maintained an apartment, in the place Dauphine.

Gigi's news had set me off; although he'd told me to keep cool, that his friend's information might turn out to be bullshit, I couldn't just sit and wait. The more I thought about it, the more agitated I became.

Yes, I was standing on the sidewalk looking up at the rather forbidding grandeur of the huge building, the uniformed *flics* buzzing and circling in their evil-looking capes like so many gossiping wasps. But no, I had not decided to throw in the towel and seek police help in finding Vivian. Not yet—not exactly.

I presented my valid passport and an old NYU identification, and I told the liaison officer my story: how I was an American law student doing a paper on police procedure in New York as compared to Paris. I would not presume to take up the time of any of the hardworking detectives on the force today, but I was wondering if he could put me in touch with an Inspector Pascal Simard, whose name I had come across in some old newspaper reportage. Surely the inspector was getting on in years now? and mightn't he have a little time on his hands these days?

Just enough of the truth, mixed with a few Nanette-type whoppers, to be believable. Or so I hoped. My reluctance to involve the authorities stemmed in part from the fear they'd discover Vivian was doing something not on the up-and-up, and the last thing I wanted to do was bring any heat down on her. On the other hand, if they embarked on some kind of investigation of *me*—so what? I had my passport, airline ticket, and ample spending money. I was staying with a nice young man in a borrowed apartment in a nice part of town and we had done nothing wrong.

I believe, based on on very few facts, the French invented bureaucracy. Were they proud of it, or embarrassed? I didn't know. But at least their red tape appeared to work, sometimes with remarkable efficiency. After the requisite number of phone calls and hours spent waiting in this queue or that anteroom—and the inevitable break for lunch—I was told that Inspector Simard, who had retired to his home in the Loire Valley, had agreed to speak to me. I was given his address and phone number in a town near Amboise, some two hundred kilometers southwest of Paris.

Andre had never actually been outside the city limits and I was letting him know how un-Parisian I thought that was. After all, you have to spend time in the provinces before you decide you hate them, right? So, wary as he was of my latest plan, he agreed to make the trip with me. First of all, Andre put no faith in anything Gigi or Martine said. He didn't believe I'd ever get that "report" on the Eiffel Tower pickpocket's tip. And second, he probably would have insisted on going with me to Simard's place anyway, to prevent me from doing anything *too* dumb. We had not been together very long, but already he had taken on the role of fool catcher: grabbing me by the shirttails and pulling me back to safety whenever my enthusiasm had me stepping off into the abyss.

We caught an early morning train at the Gare d'Austerlitz and in about two hours we were in Amboise. A local bus took us to the edge of Inspector Simard's village. We made a call to him from the *tabac*, and from there, following the good inspector's directions to the letter, we walked the velvet-plush paths until we arrived at his home.

Monsieur Simard had a full head of silky white hair under the panama hat he tipped to us when we found him in his garden. He must have been in his early seventies, but there was no suggestion of a stoop in his bearing. He was as tall and upright as Andre.

Before inviting us inside he turned to me with a questioning look on his face. "I wonder if you know any gardening secrets, mademoiselle."

"Me? Less than nothing."

"Pity," he said. "I have the feeling these flowers need more water. But then again, one doesn't want to risk drowning them, you know. I've always liked the garden so much, but it was really my wife who tended to it. I've been slowly killing off one of her prized bushes after another ever since she died ten years ago."

As he invited us inside, I thought I saw a mischievous little smile at the corner of Inspector Simard's mouth, but I couldn't be sure. So I just nodded my head in sympathetic understanding.

In less than twenty minutes I had come clean with the inspector. Simard, retired or not, had not lost his touch for eliciting confessions. I told him first about our interest in the Rube Haskins case, and this led inevitably to the saga of Aunt Vivian and my reluctance to involve the authorities. The only thing I left out was the Gigi Lacroix angle. It might be okay for me to make a clean breast of things, but I knew I had no business implicating anybody who'd been in trouble with the law.

After listening attentively to my tale, in a confession of his own he admitted, "The Haskins case is one that occasionally comes to mind. Even to this day."

"Because you never caught the murderer, you mean," said Andre.

"Yes, because of that. But I also thought every other element of the case was . . . well, one would have to say *strange*. Yes, I think that would be the word. The newspapers—and many of my colleagues, alas—either ignored this poor man's tragic death or dismissed it as a seamy sort of thing, as though Monsieur Haskins had probably lived a violent, dissipated life and could expect no more than to die terribly."

"Just how terribly did he die?" I asked. "I remember one article referring to a 'mangled' body."

"Oh, believe me, it was a vicious murder. The hatred behind it—the passion, if you will—was quite apparent. But as for your acquaintance—the old gentleman who told you that Monsieur Haskins was involved in a drunken brawl—I'm afraid he has the story all wrong.

"Monsieur Haskins, who probably was a bit drunk at the time of his death, was cornered late at night in a little cul-de-sac and struck with a car. But that was not enough for the killer. He or she ran over the body repeatedly, deliberately. It made for a revolting sight."

The inspector sniffed at the air a bit and then lit a cigarette.

My God, I found myself thinking, all that is French in a gesture. I love him.

I was captivated by the old man. Andre was, too, apparently. He couldn't seem to take his eyes off the inspector. I wondered fleetingly whether Andre would grow into a version of this elderly gentleman—part De Gaulle, part Jackson (Milt, that is, the one from the MJQ).

"No," Inspector Simard continued, "there was no evidence that Monsieur Haskins had seduced anyone's wife or been involved in anything the least bit scandalous. He had no enemies as far as I could determine. He seemed to have been a decent man. Well, let us say there was nothing to indicate he was not a decent man. The whole thing was not only a mystery but a pity. He was a performer of some reputation, you said. I've always liked and respected artists, you know."

"Don't tell me," Andre said, incredulous, "that you were a fan of Little Rube's."

"No," the inspector said, "I never heard of the man until he showed up as a file on my desk. I don't know a great deal about the American blues genre. Though I quite enjoyed the jazz I heard in New York years ago, when I was posted for a year with an anti-terrorist mission to the United Nations. I particularly enjoyed hearing Monsieur Getz at the Café Au Go Go. Tell me, is it still there?"

Andre and I exchanged amused glances. The pileup of musical coincidences was getting surreal: just last night we had discovered a cache of old vinyl in the apartment and we'd listened to Getz recorded live at the Au Go Go in 1964.

I related the story to the old gentleman, adding "Sometimes, the world seems a little too small for comfort, Inspector Simard. If you know what I mean."

"To be sure, I do."

"Let me ask you this," I said. "As I told you, we're sure that Haskins was the man whose picture we found in my aunt's book. Only she called him Ez."

"Yes."

"All right. Number two: Haskins was born in America. This thing about his being an escapee from a chain gang in the South may be true or may be apocryphal. But suppose—whatever he did or was back in the States—suppose the person who killed him was somebody from his past in America. Could be that he tracked him here. Could have been someone who had no idea Haskins was here, but he finds himself in Paris on business or vacation. And then he discovers that his old enemy Rube is living in Paris. Whatever wrong Haskins did to this person is still fresh in his mind. So he rents a car—or steals a car—or hires someone—whatever—and kills Rube Haskins and then goes sight-seeing and washes his hands of it. You never find the car that was used to commit the murder. The guy gets away scot free."

Simard smiled upon me. "All true, mademoiselle. An intelligent bit of speculation."

Andre gave my hand a quick, strong squeeze.

"At the time, my thoughts turned in a similar direction," Simard went on. "But there was a limit to how much could be done about all that. Monsieur Haskins held a Canadian passport, and the authorities there said he had no criminal record and no living relatives. Perhaps he obtained the passport with false documents—who knows? My inquiries to the United States never turned up any record of a Rube or Rubin Haskins. But then, I never knew about this possible alias of his—Ez. And of course it was impossible to check on the whereabouts and background of every American in town at the time of Monsieur Haskins's death. It was highly frustrating, you see. All those dead ends."

"And you have no memory of a woman's name coming up in your inquiries—Vivian Whatever?"

"I don't think so, no."

"Seems like this decent, humble little sharecropping poet covered his tracks very well." I sounded sour, and I meant to. "In fact, I think he did such a good job of it that perhaps he wasn't what he appeared to be. He wasn't so humble, and maybe not so decent, either."

"I agree," said Simard. "And perhaps that helped to guarantee that we would never find his killer. A mystery and a pity, *n'est-ce pas*?"

"Hmm. Listen, speaking of small worlds," I said, "I don't suppose you have an attractive older black woman working in the bakery up the road who might be my aunt Vivian, do you?"

I got my laugh out of him. Then he insisted that we stay and share the lunchtime meal he was preparing.

The inspector asked me to pick a few flowers for the table. While I was doing so, I watched Andre as he played with Monsieur Simard's two old dogs. Yep, I could see my nearsighted love—who wanted so badly to be a Frenchman—in his gray dreadlocks, a retired professor walking slowly through the village, lost in his thoughts, a few of the town children greeting him as he passed. Sitting by the fire and flipping through the books and recordings that had made him famous. Playing his violin for relaxation before he turned in. *But where am I?* Where am I in that silly daydream? Am I ten years dead, like Madame Simard? Did I die tragically in an automobile accident? Or did I simply leave him—or he me—in Paris, while we were still young?

Lunch turned out to be a near-inedible salad made with greens from his vegetable garden. The bread, however, was very good.

CHAPTER 9

PARISIAN THOROUGHFARE

"OH, WHAT A HEAD I have today, children!"

Morris Melon was drinking a fizzy concoction from the stainless-steel tumbler of the bar blender.

The old wag-scholar-expatriate was looking ragged, his big bean-shaped head lolling around on his neck.

We all took our places at the long table where the Bricktop's staff ate their supper before the doors opened for the dinner crowd.

The potatoes were superb and the steak with onions was fork tender. The collards had an indefinable Parisian spin—piquant but not too spicy. And oh those hot rolls! Taking second or possibly third helpings from the circulating platters, Andre was "boarding," as my mother says of anyone going at their food with gusto.

I got up and refilled the ice pack that Morris Melon had been pressing to the back of his neck.

"Thank you, young one." He moaned and buried his face momentarily in the cold. "Oh . . . Oh, Father, that's better."

The meal proceeded—waiters gossiping and grousing, pitchers of lemonade and tea and wine crisscrossing and changing hands. It was the idealized image of restaurant worker camaraderie. A family you choose, rather than the other way around. The kind of thing you see as a lonely teenage nerd and fasten on. It takes actually getting a job as a waitress and standing on your foots seven or eight hours at a time—not to mention the asshole customer factor—to disabuse you of your romantic notions about restaurant work. I lasted about six minutes one summer, trying to make some bucks for the next semester at school.

Old Melon, about halfway back to the land of the living, retired to his office to nap, sipping from a glass of tomato juice as he shuffled off.

Gigi Lacroix showed good timing. Andre and I had just finished our set and repaired to the bar when I was called to the telephone. The pickpocket was not just pulling his chain, after all, he said. Gigi was in Les Halles now, and we should come to meet him in the square across from the Centre Pompidou. Martine would join us for a drink.

Oh goody. The four of us back together again. I knew Andre would be overjoyed to hear it.

I snatched my man's wineglass out of his hand and began tugging at him. "Let's go."

He grumbled and fussed the whole ride on the Métro. Not only were we going to be rooked out of more money by the fatuous Gigi, he pointed out; we were heading into the nighttime carnival that is Les Halles, which was always pumping with ugly tourists and junkies and panhandlers and runaways and the dreaded wandering mimes in their cheap French sailor shirts and ghostly white makeup.

"Just where I feel like going at the end of a long day," he spat at me.

I rolled my eyes and endured it. I could endure just about anything. We were closing in on Viv!

It took ten or fifteen minutes to locate Gigi. Lady Martine was the first pointer. I saw her moving toward us, more swiftly than I ever thought possible considering the height of her heels. I damn near mistook her for one of those mimes; that's how white her face was. And her red mouth was hanging open in dumb amazement. In fact, even the wetness at the corner of her eye seemed to be frozen there, as if painted on—a comic teardrop.

I put out a hand to stop her, but she brushed right past me, moving even faster. When we began to follow, calling out her name, she became a human rocket. The night swallowed her up.

Andre and I doubled back, retracing our steps. He spotted Gigi first.

A hapless young girl with an ice cream cone, who was about to sit down and rest on the same bench Gigi was occupying, must have seen what we saw at about the same moment. Propped up against the armrest, Gigi was leaking blood from the gaping wound in his side. And those flirty, lying eyes of his: dead, dead, dead.

I caught the glint of a big thick blade on the ground.

I dug my nails into Andre's flesh so deep he nearly buckled. But we kept silent and kept right on walking.

Plop! went that ice cream. Lord, could that girl scream.

CHAPTER 10

WHAT IS THERE TO SAY?

"*NO, NO, NO!* No you're *not*! You're not going! That's only your panic talking!"

It seemed to me that he was the one who was panicking. His voice was up in the ether and his body was shaking.

"Damn right, it's panic talking," I said. "Wouldn't you say it's about time to panic? Somebody just offed Gigi."

Andre swallowed, hard, and rushed over to the refrigerator. He upended the bottle of Vittel water and didn't stop drinking until it was empty.

"I'll tell you what you oughta be doing, my brother," I said tartly. "You ought to be packing your own stuff and leaving with me."

"That is not an option, Nanette." His voice had suddenly taken on the kind of deepness you might hear in an opera, when the baritone is letting somebody know he means business. "End of discussion," he pronounced.

"Well, okay, fuck you, end of discussion."

"Okay, okay, let's try to look at things a little more calmly here, Nanette. Let's make some tea or something and talk about this."

"I don't want any stupid tea!"

He slammed the kettle into the wall and bellowed, "Then let's not fucking have any!"

That settled me down.

He began speaking very slowly, focused, oddly menacing. "What I'm trying to get at here, Nan, is this: something very bad has happened, yes. Gigi is dead, yes. But you didn't do it, and you didn't cause it. You're guilty of nothing—understand? Therefore, you have no reason to run. You have no reason to leave me."

"I'm leaving Paris, Andre, I'm not leaving *you*."

"Would you like to explain to me how you can do one without doing the other?"

"Okay, the way I put that was dumb. But you know what I meant. Look, I took on this insane project, to find my aunt, under totally false pretenses. I was bullshitting my mother and bullshitting myself—I admit that now. I thought I could use my Paris smarts to find her. That we'd have a joyful reunion and I'd give her her money and I'd eat like a king and do the museums and shop like mad and go home happy. Slick little Nan, living by her so-called wits, puts another one over on the grown-ups and lives to tell the tale. I was supposed to rescue her, get it? I never dreamed things were going to turn out like this—so weird—so horrible.

"I'm in over my head now, sweetheart. Don't you understand? The old Nanette karma has kicked in again. Even when I set out with the best intentions in the world, somebody always ends up under the old ton of bricks. I'm the world's biggest authority on turning sugar to shit. It's not just a curse; it's a talent."

I saw him trying to get in a word, but I wouldn't let him. "No, no, it's true, Andre. If I hadn't hired that oily little guy, he'd be alive today."

"There's no way on earth for you to know that," he protested, trying mightily to keep his tone even. "Gigi was a petty criminal. Maybe even not so petty. That's how he made his living. Who did he associate with: pimps, thieves. Criminals, get it? His death could have had nothing to do with you—I mean us. Hell, maybe it didn't even have anything to do with him. Look where he was hanging out. He could've just been mugged and tried to fight back. Being in the wrong place at the wrong time—that's how it is in every city in the world."

"Oh, come on. You don't really believe that."

"I don't know what to believe, Nan. I don't know what happened to him any more than you do. I just know we didn't kill him. Maybe that bitch of his did it."

"Martine did not kill that man," I proclaimed. "You saw her. You saw what she looked like. She came upon him the same way we did. And ran. The same way we did."

"All right, so she didn't do it. So she ran away. What do you think she's going to do now, accuse you? No. She wanted to get as far away from the scene as she could. People like Martine and Gigi don't go to the police. The police come to them."

"That's right. That's my point. And what's going to happen when they find her? She'll tell them about Viv. 'People like Martine' don't just grit their teeth and go off to jail. They start bargaining with the cops. They rat on their cohorts. Vivian and you and I will be implicated."

"Listen to yourself! We're not her cohorts, Nan. And why should Martine end up in jail if she didn't kill the guy?"

"Why, why, why? Stop asking me that. Why are you being so dense? Why do you refuse to see the connections between Vivian and all the absurd shit that's happened?"

"Because if there is a connection, it isn't absurd. There's a reason for it. And because I don't believe in karma. I don't believe in voodoo. I don't believe in curses. You're not a curse, Nan."

I started laughing grimly. "I'm what? A blessing?"

"Yeah. Or something like that. What else do you call it, what's happened between us?"

"Listen, Andre. I'm never going to be able to sort this out if we don't keep things separate."

"Separate?"

"Yes. Vivian. Missing. In trouble. And somehow—we don't know how, but somehow—mixed up in Gigi's killing. Rube Haskins aka Ez. Whatever his name was. Martine. All that shit on one side. And on the other side, you . . . and me."

"I'm not keeping anything separate, Nan. I've had it with being separate. The last person who 'separated' from me left me with a lousy insurance policy and my dad's Al Green records."

"Please—*please*—" I jerked away from his embrace. "Let me think!"

"Think of what, more reasons to leave?" He grabbed me again and once again I twisted out of his grip.

He stepped off from me then and removed his spectacles. I stood there in silence watching him as he polished them deliberately, compulsively, finally abandoning them on the table.

"What if I can find her?" he said at last.

"Find who?"

"Vivian. What if I find her for you? Will you stay then?"

"How are you going to do that, Andre? We've been jumping through hoops trying to find her."

"Not the right ones, obviously. We didn't do it right."

"I don't want you going to the police, Andre. Don't do it. Do you hear me?"

"What if I find Martine? What if I get her to talk—tell me who this pickpocket is who saw Vivian?"

I tried to answer him, but he wouldn't let me.

"What if I figure out who killed Rube Haskins? What if I can get the answers to these things—even just one of them—would

it be enough to make you stay? Say yes and I'll leave right now
and I will find something for you. Will you give me just one
more day and let me try?"

"Jesus Christ, man, it's two in the morning."

"Will you?"

"But—"

"Will . . . you . . . do it?"

"Yes, yes! All right."

"All right," he echoed. "Just don't pull away from me again.
Just don't, Nan." He gathered me to him, nearly crushing me.

"Andre, don't. What if something goes wrong?" I said. "If
something happens to you, what'll I do, baby? It'll kill me."

"Nothing's going to go wrong. Just stay here. Just wait. No
plane reservations, no packing, no leaving. Wait here for me.
Okay?"

I nodded yes. "Andre?"

"What?"

"Don't forget your glasses."

"GIRL, now I *know* you out of your mind!"

"I know, I know," I said wearily. "Please, Aubrey, don't bust
my chops over this anymore. I'm kind of at the end of my rope
here. Wait. Hold on a minute. I'm getting a cigarette."

I pulled the pack of filtered Gauloises and a packet of matches
from the kitchen counter and ran back to the telephone.

I hadn't even bothered to calculate what time it was in New
York. Perhaps I had awakened her in the middle of the night. Or
was it the other way around? She didn't sound sleepy, though,
and I didn't really care. I just knew I had to talk to her.

Just as Inspector Simard had done, she asked few questions,
merely listened while I recapped my activities over here and my
efforts to locate Vivian:

Taking a room at the low-rent hotel. Checking all the flea-bags in town. Checking the hospitals and the morgue. First the dueling banjos bit with Andre down in the Métro, then making friends with him. The feeling that someone had been in my room. Searching Vivian's suitcase and finding the Ez photograph and the hundred-dollar bill. Placing the ad in the *Trib*. The move to Andre's place and our playing on the street and at Bricktop's. Taking on Gigi Lacroix as a consultant. Martine's rap about the genius of Rube Haskins. The tip Gigi received about Viv. The Rube Haskins/Ez mystery. The visit to Simard. The discovery of Gigi's corpse. And finally, Andre running out into the night.

"Nanette, if I didn't know you for all these years, I wouldn't believe a word of this story," Aubrey said. "But 'cause I do, I know it's all true. Fact, you probably haven't even told me the worst of it yet. Goddammit. Other people just don't have your fucking life, girl."

Her voice had taken on that edge of maternal outrage that I both resented and craved. With Mom, I had always been so fundamentally secretive about my life that she didn't have a lot to bust my chops over. Aubrey, on the other hand, had plenty of ammunition. She not only knew in excruciating detail about all the messes I got myself into, she usually played a role in getting me out of them. Where I was a dedicated spendthrift, she was shrewd with her money. Where I tumbled time after time after time into these ensnarling, take-no-prisoners affairs with men, she was cool and guarded with her feelings, could play a man like a tin whistle, and was always the one to walk away first. My childhood friend Aubrey Davis, tough bitch that she was, was unfailingly there when I required a killer pair of high heels for the evening, a sympathetic ear for my man troubles, or simple forgiveness. In short, she had earned the motherly stance—outrage and all—she sometimes took toward me.

In a voice thick with intimidation she demanded, "And who is this Jamaican Negro you're living with, Nan?"

"He's not Jamaican. I said he had dreads. He's kind of a mulatto from Detroit and his folks are dead and—God, I wish I could tell you—I wish I could tell you everything about him." Yeah, yeah, I knew how sickening this kind of rhapsodizing could get. But I couldn't stop myself. "Like I said, I met him down in the subway. He saved me from these racist geeks. And he's just so young and sensitive and serious and I don't want to hurt him, Aubrey, I can't, I—oh, shit—I love him," I said hopelessly.

She was silent for a minute, gathering her patience, I suppose, trying to calm down, trying not to treat me as the fool she knew me to be.

"What does he look like?" she asked sheepishly.

"Child, he's so gorgeous you could die."

The both of us laughed for a long time.

"I'm not lying, girl. He's got these beautiful bony wrists and fingers and these long arms like a Watusi."

"Like a what?"

"Never mind. Let me tell you about his mouth, Aubrey. At the edges it goes down, but then it goes up again, see, like a surprise. You know what I mean? And you know how some guys have a butt that starts right underneath their waist? His is like that. And his legs are so long, they're almost as pretty as yours. And he has these humongous feet that make me want to cry when I look down at them at night, they're so—so big and awkward and the back of his ankle is so thin you don't know how he can stand up on it."

"Nan!"

"I know, I know, I know."

"You have to pack up and get out of there, girl. You could end up being tapped for that pimp's murder. The police ain't gonna hear about finding your aunt Viv. Or about Andre's butt. What are y'all going to do if they point the finger at him? If the cops over there are like they are over here, they won't look no further than the first black man they can put their hands on. They'll put his long legs *under* the jail."

That one hadn't occurred to me yet.

Since we found Gigi, I had run a whole world of horrible possibilities through the washing machine of my paranoia. For reasons I couldn't begin to explain, I felt that instead of helping Vivian I was putting more heat on her. I didn't know how; I just knew the danger to her was growing.

But I hadn't thought of the danger to Andre—Andre, who had from the very beginning wanted nothing to do with Gigi. My God, I was doing it again: I was calling down death and destruction on those I loved.

"You're right, Aubrey," I said. "I know you're right. I told Andre it was time for me to go. That we had to give up on the Vivian thing. That I had to go home. But he won't hear it. He begged me to give him another day."

"Another day for what? What's he going to find out in a day that y'all couldn't find out in two weeks?"

"Nothing, obviously. I just couldn't bear him nagging me anymore. See, for him it's not about finding Vivian. He wants me to stay here maybe permanently. He wants to . . ."

"What? What does he want?"

"I don't know. Get married, I think. Or something."

"You kidding."

"He's young, Aubrey."

"How young?"

"He was twenty-seven last month."

"That's only a year and a half younger than you are, fool."

I nodded slowly, as if she were there in the room with me.

"Nan?"

"What?"

"You not going to marry that man. I know it's good, girl. But you are not marrying a Geechee street-violin-playing Negro from Detroit. It's stupid, Nan. I don't care how cute he is, and I don't care how intelligent he is or what he does to you at night. He got his head up in the same cloud as you, Nanette. He'll never have no money, he can't take care of business, and he can't take care of you. And you belong back here."

I fell silent.

"Nan!"

"Yeah, I'm here."

"Start packing."

I began to cry, hiding it.

"I'm not playing, Nanette. Start packing."

"Right. Will you call Mom like I asked?"

"Yes, girl. Ima call her as soon as you hang up. And you gonna call me when you get a flight out."

CHAPTER 11

WHAT'LL I DO?

I FELL ASLEEP in my clothes. Everything—shoes, skirt, top, underwear.

I'd felt sorry for myself plenty of times before. I'd been in that valley of indecision and self-pity and regret more times than I cared to recall. It had never felt quite like this before.

It was a restless, heavy kind of sleep. Hideous dreams about everything from being lost in the play yard at age four to facing my father with a D in my grade book to my grandmother's ravaging cancer.

I had told Andre on that day I checked out of the hotel: I bonded with another man once in this same way—all at once, and right down to the bone. *It ended up terrible.* Be warned, young man. Black widow Nan will get you.

I heard his key in the door.

To hell with everything else. He was back.

He had been unable to find Martine, let alone Aunt Vivian. Unable to come up with anything new. I knew that he wouldn't.

You have to let yourself hope. But I knew he wouldn't. Still, he was safely back home. He looked like shit.

We cried in each other's arms. I don't even know if we knew why we were crying. And perhaps we weren't crying for the same reasons. In any case the tear fest seemed to both exhaust and reanimate us. At the end of it, he reached into his back pocket, extracted a palm-sized object of plastic, and tossed it on the table.

"What is that?" I asked.

"The total fruits of my labors," said Andre. "I asked a couple of the musicians I've met playing on the street to help me find Martine last night. We never did. But one of them found this in his girlfriend's apartment. It's an old cassette. She bought it at a flea market. And she told him it must've been some kind of joke."

"A cassette of . . . ?"

"Look at what's written there, on the front."

And so I did.

RUBE HASKINS was printed on a small piece of masking tape.

"Play it, Andre. I want to know what kind of chops this son of the South had."

He popped the tape into the player. There followed . . . nothing but a bit of static.

I flipped the cassette to its B side. Again, nothing.

We looked at each other for a long minute.

"The essential Rube Haskins," Andre said. "Bootleg, no doubt."

That sent us into not tears but hysterical laughter. Laughter that threatened to revert to tears.

He sounded like an old man: "Let's go to bed now. You have to help me get undressed. I'm too tired to do it myself."

WELL, *QUEL* MORNING.

We made love until noon—dozing, waking, doing it again,

falling off again, waking each other from bad dreams, kissing, promising.

I've had it, I thought, pulling the quilt up over my shoulders. I've had it with Little Rube the rube, I've had it with family honor and crooked Gigi and all the rest. And as for the man lying beside me, whatever he wants to do is fine by me.

Sorry, Viv.

The late afternoon bustle down in the street woke us. I'd never been so hungry in my life. I put on the coffee and Andre jumped into some clothes and went out to the market for food.

I bathed, set the table, changed the sheets, tidied the apartment, watered the plants, made a pot of coffee, drank it, and made another.

He'd been away for ninety minutes by then.

By the time another hour went by, I knew.

CHAPTER 12

POOR BUTTERFLY

I FORGOT to comb my hair, I thought, absurdly.

I bet I look like Martine, I thought. Eyes like pinwheels. Breathing through my mouth and probably drooling.

Help me! I was screaming inside my skull. *Somebody help me!*

But in reality I made no sound as I ran through the neighborhood. I was hoping for a miracle. Hoping I'd see him sitting in the café. Hoping he was waiting on line for half a kilo of ham at the market. Hoping he had run into one of his musician acquaintances or was shooting the breeze with the guy in the wine store. Hoping, even, that he'd been hit by a motorcycle and taken to the hospital with a nice, safe, lovely broken leg.

I ran blindly down into the Métro and back out again.

I went back to the apartment, still running, still hoping, still screaming inside.

No Andre.

I couldn't catch my breath. "What'll I do, baby, I'll go crazy," I wailed.

I was talking to myself.

I went on talking: "No—don't go out again. Stay by the phone. No, use the phone. Call! Call somebody."

Inspector Simard didn't answer. Where the hell was he? In that stupid garden? Drinking wine out on the lawn as the sun went down? Having coffee with the postman in the town bar? I pictured his two lazy brown dogs looking up in boredom at the ringing telephone.

I went rummaging in the liquor cabinet, knocking over a couple of those useless little cordial glasses. All I could find was a bottle of Jamaican rum. I poured out a huge glass and gulped it. No cigarettes left in the house. I pulled at my hair until my scalp ached.

Simard answered on the second try.

"Ah! *Salut, mademoiselle.* Are you well? I was thinking of you and your friend only last—"

I stopped him there and began to babble out the story in that kind of fractured French for which the Académie Française would have brought back the death penalty.

Gigi Lacroix no longer needed my discretion, my protection from the authorities. I told Simard what I'd omitted from my story before.

"That was not a very wise course to follow," he commented softly at the end of the tale.

A masterpiece of understatement.

And then he added, "It might have been better for you to have disclosed this to me during your visit."

I sighed into the receiver, not out of exasperation but grief. The sigh soon became a moan that went on forever. He hung on at the other end, making no sound except to clear his throat periodically.

"Very well, very well then," he said at last. "Listen carefully, young one. The *sûreté* will not undertake a search for Andre for at least another forty-eight hours. But you must get the wheels turning a great deal faster than that.

"I will give you the name of a lieutenant at the Quai des Orfèvres. He will contact you later, after I've had a chance to locate and speak to him. But first, go to your embassy. Do it right away. It does not matter what you tell the consul about how your friend came to be missing. The authorities are accustomed to dealing with young people in trouble. Tell them . . . Well, you are obviously adept at inventing things. Or tell them the truth, if it appears warranted. The important thing is that you go to them now. *Entendu?*"

"Yes, sir," I said, sniveling.

"Go now," he said sternly, "but first, some other advice."

"Yes?"

"I know you are a brave, independent young person, and that you are trying to do the honorable thing. But I ask you this, mademoiselle: How good an actress are you? How good are you at being a Frenchwoman?"

"What do you mean?"

"Only this: It will not do to go to the embassy, and especially not to the Paris police, as a hysteric demanding action. Present yourself as a respectable young woman, one who has taken a misstep perhaps—but a *woman*, if you take my meaning. *Une femme française.* Cry discreetly, cross your legs demurely, show how distraught you are over the disappearance of the man you love. But do not become shrill in the face of their lassitude."

Got it. The basic damsel-in-distress riff. Get the men to do what you want. Could I pull it off? Here was yet another occasion for me to wish that I was Aubrey.

On the other hand, if I wasn't genuinely in distress right now, then what in God's name could distress possibly mean?

While Simard instructed me, I began undoing my jeans and

searching the room frantically with my eyes. Where were my
pantyhose?

"Inspector?" I said.

"Oui?"

"Do you think he's still alive? Do you think I'm going to get
to him in time?"

He didn't hesitate at all. "Surely you will. You love him, *n'est-
ce pas?*"

I knew fully how little logic there was in his enigmatic answer.
Still, it was all I had, and I had to hang on to it. I rang off.

But before I could take my femme act on the road, it became
academic.

As I was wrestling horribly with the back zipper of my dress,
the telephone rang. I pounced on it, thinking, Thank you, God/
Allah/Siva/Sojourner Truth. I'd rather take my chances with
Simard's contact at the police department than face an unknown
quantity like a white American diplomat—one who, for all I
knew, might even turn out to be a woman, and what would the
sexy damsel thing get me then?

"Oui, allo!" I called into the phone.

"Nan."

It was Andre.

I fell to the floor, receiver still in my hand.

"Nan?"

"It's me, sweetheart," I said, matching the grave hush in his
voice. I willed my heart to stop pounding so loud. "Something's
wrong, isn't it?"

"Yes."

"Are you okay? I mean, not hurt."

"Yes."

"And someone's there, right? Listening. Telling you what to say."

"Yes."

"What do they want?"

"I told—" He broke off with a sharp intake of breath.

"Andre!"

"It's all right. Just listen. You know how you told me once there used to be a rape crisis center where a friend of yours was a counselor? You remember where that was?"

"Yes, I remember."

"Don't say the name of the street," he cautioned. "Just come there. Now."

"All right. I'm coming."

"Wait a minute! Come alone, right?"

"Yes."

"And bring those papers from home—from New York, I mean. You know what papers I mean, don't you? Bring all of it. You have to bring all of it, and you have to come alone, then we'll both be all right. I promise. It's not a setup, understand?"

"Okay," I said, understanding perfectly what he meant by "papers": the money I'd been sent over here to deliver. The money orders. Someone knew about my mission and was holding Andre until I turned over the money.

Of course, I thought, it had to be the Gigi/Martine underworld connection. I had been stupid enough to go to a petty crook for help, and now I was reaping the wages of that error.

Except I had not been stupid enough to tell them the reason I was looking for Vivian was to turn over an inheritance to her. I'd never said a word to Gigi or Martine or anyone but Inspector Simard about the ten thousand. Yet somehow they'd found out.

I was betting Gigi had been killed because of that money.

"Understand everything now?" Andre asked.

The answer to that one, obviously, was no. But that isn't what I said.

"Yes" is what I said. "I'm on the way." I started to ask once more if he was okay, but I realized I was speaking into dead air.

———

THE STREET HE would not let me name was a little cul-de-sac in the 11th, off the rue Chanzy. There is such a thing as the beaten path. There's off the beaten path. And then there is Cité Prost—that's the street Andre was talking about.

I had indeed once known someone who volunteered her time at a women's counseling center there. Andre and I had dropped another musician off in a cab one night and I had pointed the old building out to him.

"Kind of an isolated part of town for something like that, isn't it?" he asked.

"If you think it's weird now, you should have seen it then," I said. "When you went in for rape counseling, you were always looking over your shoulder to make sure somebody wasn't going to rape you."

THERE WAS STILL a slice of sunlight left when I emerged from the Métro. The rosy horizon lit my way as I trotted along the avenue, looking for the sharp turn into Cité Prost.

I found it, made the turn, and then halted in my tracks. The grimy street hulked before me like a living presence, a fearsome thing with hollow eyes and wings.

Half the buildings on the street had been razed. Half of those remaining were in some stage of gentrifying refurbishment. Piled building bricks, wheelbarrows, and construction machinery cluttered the sidewalks.

The women's center was all boarded up. I stood on the pavement and waited, staring at the building. Was I expected to go in? My heart froze in my chest. How was I going to get in? I looked around for the inevitable *type* who would emerge from the shadows and take me around the back way. Who else would be inside? Homesteading addicts fixing by candlelight? Lady Martine in her stilettos, the ringleader of some murderous band of outsiders? She was surely not to be discounted as a party to this extortion.

Where did they have Andre? The thought of him gagged and locked in a closet or in a corner with his wrists and ankles bound made me furious and paralyzed, by turns. I tried not to think the worst—that they had killed him as soon as he hung up, as soon as I'd agreed to bring the money—but I was losing the battle.

What if they were watching me right now? Killing him right now?

The press of all those gruesome possibilities was too much. I began to rush toward the building. But a word spoken softly and carried on the mild air stopped me.

"Nan."

I whirled.

Not another soul on the street. I looked around frantically. Up at the bricked-in windows. Even to the branches of a yellowing plane tree. Where had that voice come from?

There was an old gray Volkswagen parked directly across from the center. I hadn't even noticed it before. I walked toward it, slowly. That was Andre sitting behind the wheel. He lifted one hand slightly and beckoned me to him.

I ran to the driver's side and tried to open the door.

"Take it easy, Nan," he said tonelessly. "Go around to the other side and get in."

For a moment I couldn't move to obey him. I was too busy searching his face for bruises, checking his clothing for bloodstains. But then I saw him wince, and he repeated sharply, "Go around and get in, Nan."

I did it on the double.

"Don't turn around yet!" he barked when I had closed the door after me.

It soon became plain what his wincing was all about. There was a gun less than half an inch from the nape of his neck.

"I'm *okay*, Nan, just you be cool," he said, seeing me seeing the black muzzle.

A *titter* came from the back seat then, no other word for it, really. Yeah, a titter. Tinkling and merry, and perhaps tinged with madness.

"Yeah, he's okay," said the laugher. "And you know what, girl? I want to thank you for letting me borrow this pretty man of yours for the day. We had a lot of fun."

Andre's warnings be damned. I turned around and took a good look. A good hard look.

A silence had fallen in the car. It went on and on and on. I was the one to break it.

"Vivian," I said, "I hate you."

CHAPTER 13

YOU'VE CHANGED

"I MEAN, I hate what you're doing. Whatever that is."

"I swear to Jesus," she replied, "sometimes I barely know what I'm doing anymore."

"Here's a suggestion," I said. "Get that gun away from Andre's head. Are you out of your mind!"

The thing was withdrawn, and Andre let out an endless breath. I took his hand and held it for a long moment before turning back to my sweet old aunt, as Gigi had once called her.

"I'm not sure you heard me, Viv. I just asked you if you were out of your mind."

Vivian sighed heavily, then, as if she'd just had a hit of B_{12}, demanded breezily, "Where's that money, Nanny Lou? Pretty here tells me my ship's come in. When I found out you were in Paris looking for me, I figured you'd brought some dough from home. But I never dreamed you were going to make me rich."

It was my turn to laugh. "Just a minute here, Aunt Viv. Let

me get something straight first. You think you can frighten my mother half to death with your stupid telegrams, get me all the way over here, and then, like, *hide* from me—terrorize me—kidnap my fucking boyfriend and hold us at gunpoint. Then you're gonna call me Nanny Lou, right? Like when you used to bounce me on your knee. Do I have all that right, Aunt Viv?"

"I never bounced you on my knee, girl."

"You know what I'm saying, Vivian."

"Yes, I do. I'm something else, huh?" she said soberly.

She leaned forward a bit. There was gray in her hair now, and her eyes were dull, the coppery skin over her thin face not so taut anymore. But she was still my wild auntie. Great bones, high forehead, wide and noble nose with that sexy bump between the nostrils. Still a package of sharp angles and nervous energy. My dad's wayward sister. My babysitter and role model whom I adored. Aunt Vivian. Armed kidnapper and holdup woman.

I couldn't take it in. "Why'd you do it? Why?"

"That makes no difference now. I know I scared you shitless, and I'm sorry I had to do it this way. But for one thing, I can't have you running all over town with my name on your lips. And for another, I want that money, Nan. You give me that money and then you and your young man get on a plane and go home, you understand me? Get out of Paris. This has nothing to do with you, and you're going to get burned bad if you stay here."

"Nothing to do with us?" Andre at last spoke up. "Lady, you've been threatening to blow my head off for several hours now, but you can sit there and say it has nothing to do with us?"

She didn't answer him, head turned away.

He finally exploded. "I ought to come back there and snatch you bald."

I managed to shush him with a hand to his face.

"Who was Ez?" I asked, sudden, point-blank.

Snap of the head. "What?" Her voice broke.

"You heard me. Who was Ez? The man who also called himself Little Rube Haskins. And what do you know about the way he died?"

"I'm not going to talk to you all about that. I told you, that's nothing to do with you!" She was gripping the back of my seat tightly as she spoke.

"You heard what Andre just said. If it didn't have anything to do with us, we wouldn't be sitting here looking down the barrel of a gun. So cut the shit, Auntie. I want to know what's going on here. I want some answers. Were you sleeping with that guy Haskins when you lived in Paris all those years ago? Did you set him up to be killed?" It frightened me to ask the next question, but I did anyway: "Did you run him down yourself?"

Her fingers tightened on the old upholstery.

"Why did you run from your hotel, and why did you make yourself so hard to find? Who told you I was looking for you?" I pressed.

No answers. Just an awful grimace and her knuckles going white.

I screamed out my next question: "Did you know a pimp named Gigi who was murdered the other day? Don't just sit there like a mummy, Vivian. You owe me some answers! And don't give me any more of that shit about getting burned. We're already burning."

"All right, Nan, that's enough!" She returned my nasty tone at equal volume. "Stop playing tough, because you don't scare me. There are much nastier guys than you after my ass. And they don't just want to make me apologize for not dropping a line every once in a while. They want me dead."

"Who?" Andre said before I got the chance. "Who wants you dead? Jesus Christ, woman, why don't you just tell us what this is about?"

Vivian flinched at his tone. And then she almost smiled. "All right. Listen up, the both of you. I'm going to tell you as much as you need to know and hope it's enough to convince you to get out of town." She turned those now-sad brown eyes on me.

"I had me a lot of fun back in the day. A lot of friends and a lot of coke and a lot to drink—and a lot of men. This one particular one," she said slowly, "your father used to call a cracker. To his face. He thought that was funny. But then, as you know, my brother never had much of a sense of humor.

"I don't know why, exactly, don't ask me to explain it, but this one I loved. Jerry Brainard was his name. I don't know if you remember him."

"Kind of," I said. "We found his picture in your album."

She nodded. "You're young, baby. Both of you are. You don't know yet what it does to you when somebody you thought loved you turns around and puts a knife in you. I don't just mean leaving you. I don't mean hitting you or screwing around on you or anything like that. I mean when you love them enough to give them your eyes, and then they actually put you in a position where—where you could actually die. They could've saved you. But they didn't. You just don't know what that kind of betrayal is like."

I had to fight myself to keep from interrupting her, to tell her that, young or not, I'd had an almost identical experience with a man I thought I loved. But I couldn't go into that now. I had to hear *her* ghost story now.

"When we were living here in Paris, it was fabulous," Vivian said, coming alive again for just a second. "I was over here—speaking French, girl! I had this fine man who was crazy about me and a lot of other men in love with me and all the good times in the world and the party never stopped. Just like back at home. Just like everywhere in those days. Your aunt Viv could hang with the best of them and drink most men under the table. Baby, I was out there."

"I know," I said.

"Well, the day came when the party *did* stop. Jerry screwed me royally. Left me—what do they say?—twisting in the wind. But hey, those are the breaks, right? Somebody dogs you like that, it's cold, yeah, but you can walk away in one piece.

"But that wasn't the worst of it, not by a long shot. See, there was this other fella who was crazy about me, too. This Negro loved me in a way I couldn't begin to understand at the time. And I played him something shameless."

"You mean Ez. Rube Haskins."

"Yeah. Ez. A sweet little guy who was in way over his head. I let him think I could have the same kind of feelings for him that he had for me. All to help Jerry. I'm not proud of it, Nan. I did a lot of stuff I never should have done—things you'd be ashamed to know about me—but I feel worst about Little Rube. Because he ended up . . ."

"Dead. He was murdered," I supplied.

"Yeah, that's right."

"Jerry kill him?"

She nodded. "It ripped me apart when I heard about it."

"Until you got to the next party," Andre said.

Vivian shot him a bullet of a look. But she didn't deny his words. "That was all a long time ago," she continued. "I did what I had to do to survive. A lot of the stuff I did wasn't very nice. Wasn't the kind of news my family would appreciate hearing. But I never forgot Ez, I never forgot Jerry, and I never forgave.

"I'm about played out now, Nan. Look at me. Do I look like I'm still a party girl? You think all the pretty men still want me? Think anybody wants to use my picture to sell nylons or a pack of cigarettes? I don't think so.

"But now I see my chance to get even. To even the score—for me and for Ez. A couple of months ago I heard through some people I know that Jerry was living in Paris again. I decided to come over here and see him, see him one more time—and kill him. I've got to kill him, understand, because he's still at it. Even after all this time he's still trying to bury me."

And Daddy had once voiced the fear that "maybe" Vivian was "accepting money from men." I had to laugh at the memory.

My fabulous aunt Vivian. Next time I should be a little more careful about choosing a role model.

I shook my head. "You can't do it, Viv," I said. "It doesn't work that way, sadly. You *can't* get even."

"Watch me," she said, then corrected herself: "No, don't watch me. That's what I'm trying to tell you and this boy. Get out of here so you don't have to watch me. So none of it touches you."

Too late for that.

"What did you mean—that thing about burying you? You mean he knows you're in Paris and coming after him?"

"Yeah, he knows all right. A piece of scum he sent after me almost killed me one night. If I hadn't been carrying a can of Mace, I wouldn't be here talking to you now. I spotted the same guy hanging around my hotel, waiting for a rematch. Oh yeah, he knows I'm here all right.

"A couple of weeks ago the bastard killed someone else. Or had her killed. A white girl from the States. And the son of a bitch is trying to tie me to it. He's playing some kind of sick game with me. The globe that was used to bash in that child's skull? That was mine. I've been carrying it around forever. It belonged to my mother. It was in the suitcase in my room, along with some jewelry and old photographs and whatnot. I can't remember half of what I had in that bag. See what I mean about him? He ain't no regular motherfucker. He's Satan.

"I'll be getting even, all right. I'm going to kill him. And after that—whatever happens, happens. If I make it out of town, fine. If I don't, fine. But I don't want you here. I don't want you to have to deal with the fallout."

I went back to that morning when Andre and I sat on the hotel bed amid the breakfast dishes, reading about Mary Polk's murder in the morning paper. I recalled the cold ripple that had gone up my back.

Thank God, I thought then, thank God it isn't Viv lying dead in that alley. I had tossed the newspaper aside and never spoke of the story again. But that killing had worried me, even then. Maybe it was something as ethereal as that little square of fabric on the ground, the one that had indeed been Vivian's Scout bandanna. I don't know. But something had made me fear the murder was no out-of-the-blue occurrence, a tragedy unconnected to our lives. I felt somehow that it did have something to do with us—with Vivian and me. And that it was going to come back on us one day.

"Back up a minute," Andre was saying to Vivian, trying to sound soothing. I knew what he was going to ask her, 'cause I had the same question for her on the tip of my tongue. "The girl from the States. What was she doing with him?"

Vivian snorted. "I don't know what that chick was doing with him—or for him. It could have been any one of a hundred things. He had a way of working people. Before you knew it, you were in the middle of his shit."

"Did you ever help him in any of his—his—*ventures* when you were with him? Did he work you?"

Her stiff posture and the way she bit off her words before uttering them gave me my answer.

My role model had done a bit of everything, it seemed. The pickpocket, whoever he was, the one who made the cryptic remark about Viv being up to her old tricks? Guess he hadn't lied. Whatever he meant by the remark, it didn't matter anymore.

What mattered was shutting my aunt down before she blew away this Satan of an ex-husband and spent what was left of her life in prison. She would be better off just telling the police that

Brainard killed Rube Haskins. Rat him out. If they reopened the case and could prove that, she'd have her revenge. If the law in France worked the same way it did in the States, there was no statute of limitations on murder. They could, theoretically, nab you a hundred years after the fact.

Inspector Simard would help us, I was certain, advise us. Viv had done something awful to Rube Haskins; she had used him, but that's not murder. That was the main thing: she'd had nothing to do with the murder.

Now, how was I going to get her to see it that way?

I'd done my share of dumb things, and God knows I play fast and loose with the truth when it suits my purposes. But I tell myself that I still have a fairly good heart; at any rate, whatever there is in my heart, it ain't larceny. I have a salty tongue sometimes, I'm told. But I'm not a cynic, either. Something beautiful, new, intriguing, sexy presents itself to me, my first instinct is to say yes rather than no.

I had always thought Viv had a lot to do with me being that way. That my determination to be "out there," as she put it, was due to her influence. Now I wasn't so sure. I just knew she was family, she was in trouble, and I had to help her.

"I want my money, Nan."

"Okay," I said, stalling. "Tell us where Jerry is now. Do you know where to find him?"

"I'm not telling you nothing. How stupid do you think I am, Nanette?"

"Honestly, Viv? I don't know how stupid you are. Excuse me for pointing it out, but you're about to embark on one stupid-ass course of behavior. You've had it bad for a long time, it sounds like. But now you've got ten grand, like a gift from God, and all you can think to do is go to prison for murder. Why don't you rat Jerry out to the cops and then go get yourself a room at the Ritz and start living? Fuck revenge."

"I have my own reasons for doing it this way," she said icily.
"Hand over that money."

"All right. Just a minute. Just answer one thing more."

"What?"

"Why on earth did you write home to Mom asking for help—
telling her you were broke and stranded?"

"Andre asked me the same thing," she said impatiently. "I
already told him. I *was—am*—broke and stranded. But I didn't
write jack to your mother. I don't know what the hell you all are
talking about."

"Then it had to be Jerry who sent the card and the telegram,"
Andre reasoned.

"That's right," I echoed. "He's been setting you up for something for a while now, Vivian. He's just playing with you. He
must've known where you were long before you knew where he
was. Why don't you face the fact that you're not going to win
this game with him? He's going to—"

"I'm through talking, Nan. Give me those checks."

"Vivian, you're not going to put that gun on us again. . . . Oh.
I guess you are."

"You think I want to, girl? You're making me do it! Just give
me the money and stop asking questions!"

I did as she asked.

"All right, Andre," she instructed, "leave the keys, and you
get out."

Frantic, he began to splutter: Where was she taking me? Why
couldn't he go, too? If she was going to commit murder, that
was her business, but why did she have to take me down with
her?

"Just . . . get . . . the . . . fuck . . . out. Nan's not going any-
where with me. She's getting out, too."

I climbed out wearily and joined Andre on the sidewalk, Vivian's gun trained on his heart.

"The two of you get over there in the doorway of that old building. And don't move until I drive away."

"One last time, Viv—"

"I told you, Nanette. I'm through talking. Move!"

We backed over to the abandoned women's center.

"Forget it," I heard Andre say as I craned my neck to read the back license plate. "She covered up the back one. I never got a look at the front."

We heard the engine turn over.

"You're on the way to the guillotine, Viv," I shouted to her. I made a knife-across-the-throat gesture.

"They haven't used a guillotine in decades," she yelled back.

"Hey! Hey, Viv! What do you need that money for?"

She leaned over and her face appeared for a moment through the open window on the passenger side. "I need to buy a gun."

Andre and I looked at each other in puzzlement.

"Here, baby!" she called, sounding young and merry again. "Go play with your toys."

A second later we heard the dull clatter of a metal object hitting the pavement. Then the car zoomed off.

I ran over and picked up the weapon, which was, despite its weight, nothing more than a prop—like she'd said, a toy.

The Volkswagen was nowhere in sight. No, it wouldn't be. I recalled how Viv had this one boyfriend whose car she would borrow sometimes, a cute red convertible. She drove incredibly fast, like a demon. Cut quite a figure behind the wheel with her pretty hair blowing against the wind.

CHAPTER 14

DO NOTHING TILL YOU HEAR FROM ME

THE *GARDIEN* for the apartment building told us a police detective had come by to see me. The detective had left his card and asked me to phone him at the station the moment I got back.

I put the card in my pocket and followed Andre up the stairs and into the apartment.

So my big, strong man—the love of my life—had been held hostage for five hours by an unarmed hundred-and-some-pound middle-aged lady.

I wanted to laugh.

But I didn't. I was too tired. And too grateful he was alive. And too mad at Vivian.

I borrowed another phrase from the late Gigi Lacroix. "So you thought you were looking up the ass of death, huh?" I asked Andre. "What was going through your mind? Were you praying? Did you curse the day you met me?"

"Praying that her finger didn't slip," he said quietly. "And I cursed all right. But not you. Your aunt—" The words seemed to fail him there. "God, that bitch is crazy."

He collapsed into the nearest chair and I poured him a stiff drink of the rum I had been guzzling a few hours earlier.

"I don't suppose there's anything to smoke in the house," he asked leadenly.

"I ran out of Gauloises."

"No, Nan. I mean something to *smoke*. If ever two people in the world deserved to get high, it's us."

I walked away from him and settled in the chair on the other side of the room. "Listen," I said, "I know what you must be thinking."

"Thinking about what?"

"About Vivian. Deciding what to do."

"Do?"

"Yes. I know you've had it. You're just grateful that you've still got a head on your body. All you want to do is wash your hands of Vivian. And I don't blame you, believe me."

"Wash my hands! Nan, she just blew us off. Like you told her, she kills that guy and her problems are just beginning. There's no decision for us to make except who to call first—the cops or the men with the white lab coats and the Thorazine. Vivian's not responsible anymore. She has to be stopped."

"I know that!" I said impatiently. "Yes, of course she has to be stopped. But not by the police. I've got to get her out of here and back home where she can get some help."

"Don't you start with that shit again, Nanette. I'm telling you."

"Andre, what do you want me to do? Do you want me to call the police and report she's running around with a real gun now?"

"Yes. And you know what else? I want you to stop fucking around in this mess so we can live the rest of our lives."

"Andre, if she goes around waving a gun, they'll cut her down without blinking. She's not responsible anymore. You said it yourself."

"I'm not going to argue with you about this, Nan. Call that detective. Or call Simard. Just do it. But you can't go around like the angel of justice, saving the day for everybody—for your mother, for Vivian, for this bastard Jerry, for dead people even. You got your hands full just barely keeping yourself in one piece—and I mean just."

"Well, thank you so much, Andre. I'm an incompetent, right? And an egomaniac along with it."

"I give up." He dismissed me with a gesture of disgust.

"What—I'm supposed to talk to the hand now?"

He turned his back to me and snapped on the tape player. "We could do with some silence. Let's just have the peaceful sounds of Little Rube Nothing."

As before, a whole lot of nothing emanated from the speakers.

I went over to the refrigerator and began searching for food I knew damn well we didn't have.

"This must be Martine's fave," Andre said in a whisper. " 'The Field Hand's Prayer.' "

He was laughing evilly at his own wit. Then he began to pontificate, sadistically, scatologically, on what he'd like to do to Martine and every condescending, ignorant black music manqué like her.

I wasn't laughing, though. I was pacing the length of the apartment.

"Andre?"

"Huh?"

"Shut up."

"Huh?"

"I've got to make a call."

———

"INSPECTOR SIMARD? It's Nan Hayes."

"*Oui.* What has happened? Did you see my young friend from the prefecture?"

"I'll tell you about that in a minute," I said. "First of all, Andre is safe. He's here, with me."

"I am relieved."

"Yes. Me too. Now I have to ask you something else. I know it sounds strange, but please just tell me. It's important."

"If I can, young one. What is it?"

"Do you recall, Inspector, when you were working the Rube Haskins case, if there was ever any mention of the name Jerry Brainard?"

There was a long silence. When at last he answered *non*, it seemed to be with great hesitation; that one-word answer was heavy with meaning.

"Why did you say it that way, Monsieur Simard? Please tell me. Do you recognize the name or not?"

"Actually, yes, I do."

"You mean he was questioned in the murder investigation?"

"No, never. He had no connection to the Haskins investigation. I know that name for quite a different reason. Brainard was well known to the police. He was suspected of counterfeiting as well as of other crimes, large and small. But we were unable to put him away. He associated with a host of known criminals, but we were never able to catch him at anything. Tell me why you are asking about this man."

"Because my aunt—because Andre and I know now that he was my aunt's husband. Vivian and Brainard involved Haskins in something. I don't know what it was, but it was pretty bad. Then Brainard deserted her. He killed Rube Haskins. And it's likely he killed Gigi Lacroix as well."

"*Comment?* He did what?"

"It's true, Inspector. And now we've got to do something before he ruins another life."

"Are you certain? Was it your aunt who told you this?"

"Well, yes. And no. I mean—please tell me, what are you holding back?"

"Mademoiselle Hayes, Brainard evaded the law for many years. But I don't see how he could cause ruin to anyone at this time, or ever. He's been dead for a long while. He was murdered a few days before Mr. Haskins's death. A security agent found him in an automobile parked in the arrivals lot at Orly Airport. He'd been shot in the back of the head."

"But that can't be. It can't."

"I assure you, it's quite true. I was not assigned to the case, but of course I was notified. The team in charge of the investigation believed one of his criminal cohorts must have executed him."

Vivian had just told us she'd been in Paris for a couple months. If that was true, she had to know Jerry was dead. How could she not know? She distinctly said she knew where Jerry Brainard was right now—that she was going to get him as soon as she obtained a weapon. It meant she was chasing a man she knew was dead. Taking her revenge on a dead man.

I hung on to the receiver a long time, trying to digest this latest news, my mind racing as it grabbed hold and then let go of one slippery fact after another; tried to sort out the sane from the insane; figure out who was unhinged and who was merely a liar.

"What's he saying? *What's he saying?*"

I batted Andre away from me.

"Hello—mademoiselle?" the inspector called.

"Yes, yes," I snapped, rude as could be. "I have to go now."

"*Ne quittez pas, mademoiselle!* Don't hang up yet! Have you seen my friend from the department? If you know anything about any of these murders, you must tell him."

"Yes, yes, yes. I'm going to see him right now," I said, and hung up. Big lie.

"WHAT DO YOU MEAN, you feel like a drink?"

"Just that, Andre. Let's go get a drink. Please, let's just go *now*!"

"You must have caught something from Vivian. She's talking about killing a man she must know is already dead. And you—with the French police looking for us and Vivian out there with a weapon—you want to go have a nice drink somewhere."

"You got it. No more questions now, lamb-pie. Move it."

CHAPTER 15

WHAM BEBOP BOOM BAM

"I DON'T GET IT," I muttered, looking around. "Where is everybody?"

Jacques waved at us. He was the assistant manager at Bricktop's.

"*Ca va?*" he asked.

"*Oui*, I'm fine, Jacques. How come the place is so empty tonight?"

"It's Tuesday," he explained.

"Yeah, so what?"

"Everyone goes to Parker's on Tuesday. Even Monsieur Melon. Tuesday is new talent night over there. Monsieur Melon never misses new talent night at Parker's. He finds the best young musicians there and asks them to perform here. Just like you and Andre."

"YOU NEED HELP, NAN. You've lost your mind, do you know that?"

Andre was speaking through a mouthful of the chestnut crêpe that he had grabbed on the run from Bricktop's to the Métro.

Parker's was back in the 5th, not ten minutes away from our place on the rue Christine.

"I can't explain it yet," I kept telling Andre. Not *all* of it. Because a couple of pieces were still missing. And without those pieces, the rest was—well, inexplicable. The important thing was to get to Parker's right away, to act now, before something irreversible happened.

When we strode through the double doors of the impeccably smoky, low-lit club, I may have looked sure of myself. I wasn't. In truth, I didn't know what was going to happen—or even if. Maybe Andre was right and I was loco, tripping again. But what if the evil *if*s stirring around up there in my brain were all true? I had to do something. This was my last chance.

A girl singer in Carmen McRae capri pants and a button-down white shirt was just finishing the last chorus of "The Devil and the Deep Blue Sea."

The emcee announced intermission and a curtain of conversational babble descended, almost covering the taped music (Wayne Shorter, live, 1964) they had begun to pipe in. The voguing, profiling, and table-hopping started then. Folks moving around, floating through the place like minnows. Black-clad Euros, white Yanks with black ladies, black Yanks with blondies, and a healthy measure of prosperous Japanese in drop-dead designer clothes. Not a bad-looking crowd.

With the flummoxed Andre trailing behind me, I made my way across the packed room to the brass-railed bar. I began to scan the crowd. If there had been any doubt before, now I knew Andre was freaked out, off his game, because I spotted the celebrated American jazz musician at a table near the stage before he did.

"What are you looking at, Nan?"

"Not 'at.' 'For.' "

"Okay. What are you looking for?"

"I'm not sure. Let's get a drink."

We ordered and I continued to look around.

"Comfortable now?" Andre was patronizing me, attempting to push me down on a barstool, a controlling hand in the small of my back.

I didn't bother to answer. I just nodded, craning my neck to take in every corner of the room.

"Boy oh boy, I hope De Gaulle answers my letter," Andre said, testing me to see whether I was paying any attention to him.

I laughed and took his hand and kissed it quickly, then returned it to him.

"Who's this on the tape now," I asked, "doing 'High Fly'?"

"Jaki Byard. Like you don't know."

Andre downed a good half of his wine along with a fistful of cashews. "I never liked that guy, you know?" he said in a confessional tone, nodding discreetly toward the famous musician. "I always felt bad about it, not liking him, I mean. But I just don't. He's a smug little prick."

Well, this was good. Andre was getting distracted from what he considered my mental breakdown. He was also getting a little drunk. Understandable, since he hadn't eaten in days. I was fighting a hunger headache of my own. He polished off the nuts and then dug in on the basket of pretzels.

"There's that couple," Andre said, pointing to an elderly man and woman not far from us. "You know, they always give us a hundred francs at Bricktop's."

"Yes, they're nice people," I agreed, not looking.

"I wonder if I should try to interview them sometime. They're not black, but they are Americans who've been over here for something like forty years. Maybe they could fill in a few blanks for me. Maybe they knew some people I can't quite nail in that chapter on the fifties."

"Good idea," I said, still searching the room. I signaled the bartender for refills.

"I guess Jacques didn't lie about all the Bricktop's people being here. Those actors who always come in late are here, too," Andre noted. One of the women in the troupe was waving at us—well, at Andre. I knew what that was about.

"I bet I know what all this is about, Nan," he said a few minutes later. He was grinning like a Cheshire.

"What?" I said.

"This is some kind of complicated surprise. Everybody in here knows. I'm the only one out of the loop. Is that it? Some eminence is just about to walk in, and I'm going to be totally knocked out. Right?"

I looked at him. Be careful what you wish for, is what I was thinking. "Sweetie," I said, "I wish that was true."

"Then what the fuck is it, Nan? You expecting somebody from your wild past?"

"Just be patient a little longer." I begged. "Hang in there. I almost have it figured out, Andre. Have some more wine."

"No problem if you're looking for Morris," he said. "There he is—over there."

Yes. On the far side of the room Melon was holding court, as usual, the center of attention in his fraying London-tailored jacket. He and four other people were hunched around a little pin dot of a table and the old man was serving up some obviously tasty star-filled gossip. And, like always, the drinks were flowing nonstop. Lots of raucous laughter. Looked like a good time was being had by all.

"Nan, I've had it. You tell me what's going on, and tell me right now."

"Okay," I said, "I'm going to try to. But keep looking around while I'm talking."

"Look around for what, girl?"

At that very moment, my eye had fallen on a female server. Not a young person like all the others. And not wearing the ubiquitous white apron. She was walking briskly across the length of the club, tray in hand.

"The waitress—" I said slowly. I broke off there.

"What waitress?"

I grabbed his head and turned it toward the woman.

"The waitress, Andre! That woman with the tray!"

I meant the one with the automatic weapon resting next to the highball glasses. Vivian still had nice taste. She had chosen something in understated gray—very sleek, very expensive-looking, and definitely not a toy.

"That's Vivian! She's going to kill him!"

I leapt off the barstool and began to rush toward Morris Melon's table. "Stop her, Andre!" I screamed as I ran. "It's Vivian! Stop her!"

Viv let the glass-laden tray fall to the floor with a crash. The important item on the tray, the gun, she was now holding with both hands as she strode like the Jolly Green Giant, closer and closer to Melon.

He and his party were so high, and so wrapped up in their own fun, they had paid no attention to the shattering glass. But now, with screams breaking out all over the place as one by one the patrons spotted Viv and realized what was happening, Melon was turning in the chair, bringing his chest full into Vivian's line of fire. He might as well have been wearing a bull's-eye on his breast.

Still a few feet away from him, I already had my arm extended so as to grab the back of his collar and pull him to the floor.

Andre was closing in on Viv using the same MO. I heard him call her name. I know she must have heard him. But she never broke stride.

The old man had bounded out of his chair before I could reach him. The others in his party were diving for cover—uselessly. Those little tin café tables wouldn't have provided decent cover for a tadpole.

The first shot rang out then, roaring past the clumsily moving Melon and exploding a glass-fronted cabinet.

Melon tried a serpentine footballer's move. Pitiful. Loping like an old dog. *Pitiful*—it was almost funny.

More screams. We were in it now.

But then, switching tactics, Melon suddenly turned back to face Vivian. He raised his arms, begging, as if a heartfelt plea was going to stop her next bullet.

Everyone seemed to freeze then, waiting for what would come next.

"Listen to me, Vivian!" Melon cried out.

Vivian broke into hideous laughter. "I finished listening to you a long time ago, Morris."

He swallowed with great effort, his eyes going neon.

Another shot. *Whang!* It went into an amp up onstage. That caused a sort of Vietnam War–movie *boom* that seemed to shake the club to its foundation. The people rolling around on the floor were now trying to cover their ears as well as their asses.

Melon limped on. Looking for shelter. Hollering.

Before she got off the third shot, Andre was on her. They twisted and lurched together, both of them keening and cussing as they struggled for the gun.

As I took the first step toward them, the gun began to splutter madly. I ducked, then began to crawl toward them through the bedlam.

Another burst of bullets. And then I heard Andre's roar of shocked pain.

I stood up just in time to see him go down, blood on his shirtfront.

I tried to rush Vivian, but it was no good. With a clear field now, she was aiming at Morris Melon's back, and she sent out a long, clean volley straight into him. He crumpled at the mouth of the small kitchen.

What the hell did I think I was doing? I went for her, screeching, my hands out like cat's claws.

"Get back!" she commanded, the gun now on me. "It's over, Nan. Get back!" She was shaking so hard I almost took the gamble of reaching for the weapon.

Over. How right she was.

I heard myself repeat the words I had uttered to her in the Volkswagen: "I hate you, Vivian."

Through a flood of tears she tried to say something.

I heard Andre moan deeply then and fell on my knees beside him. When I looked up again, Vivian had disappeared.

While the crowd scattered like frightened cockroaches, I covered Andre with my body, begging no one in particular to get help, and to let him live.

A minute or two later I heard a muffled explosion outside the walls of the café. A single burst of gunfire.

Yeah. I knew that was coming, too.

How else could something like this end?

CHAPTER 16

I WANT TO
TALK ABOUT YOU

I HAD TO GO. Soon. Vivian was rotting in the municipal hospital.

Luckily, I was free to suffer the agony of all the hard deci-
sions I had to make from the relative luxury of the rue Christine.
Thanks to Monsieur Simard's friend in the department, I wasn't
in a jail cell on an obstruction charge.

My last look at my once-beloved aunt was a horror show. She
lay all curled into herself on the stones out behind the kitchen
of Parker's. Most of her face was gone. Deal with that. I'd never
seen anything worse. Yet all I could think was: My God, how
little she looks—she must be so lonely. But touch her? No.
Nuh-uh. She was family, my father's flesh and blood; she and I
had loved each other once; and I knew I'd forgive her someday
for all the pain and mayhem she had caused. But I would not
touch her. I know I should have found some way to say good-bye
to her. I guess I could have prayed over her, or something, but I
didn't. I was stupefied by then and I had to get to the hospital
to be with Andre.

On the piano at Parker's, they found a letter addressed to me. The message was less a suicide note than a cryptic kind of poem, an elegy:

Nanette—

Forgive all the lies. But that's what liars do. So now I've got only one truth to give you. Six months ago. As usual, I've got a job not worth having and a man not worth the trouble—but a damn sight better than me. They tell me at the clinic I got cancer and nothing they can do about it. Nothing I can do, rather.

Traveling Viv, always on the move. I say to myself, Girl, it's time for one last trip. Time to make amends. Time to put it all to rest. And time for payback.

A lot of thinking about it all. Everything I did and everything I didn't do. My father. Your father. And the rest of the stupid parade. Out of all of them, only one person really loved me. At least, that's what I thought. It turned out that two loved me. The little one never did make up his mind what side of the fence he should be playing on. But that didn't matter. As for Jerry, he was what he was, I knew that from the get, and he did the best he could by me. I was the one who lost faith, not him.

Jerry said he was going for a big score. Something that was going to net us more than $100,000. But he needed help. He needed another man for the job, and it had to be someone he could trust. Ez was afraid though. So I was supposed to talk him into it. Persuade him any way I could.

I was scared too. I knew it had to be something dangerous and no doubt something criminal, but I didn't ask questions. I went to work on Ez, you can imagine how, and he finally agreed to do it.

Jerry didn't want me to be here when it went down. He wanted to keep me safe. He bought me a ticket. I was to go to Lisbon and wait for him. And I did. I went and I waited. And waited. I was half crazy with worry. Knew something must have gone terribly wrong and they'd been caught. Frightened the police might be looking for me too. I wasn't supposed to let anybody know where I was. But I couldn't take it any longer. I took a chance and called Morris, asking if he knew where Jerry was. He didn't, he said. He hadn't seen him for weeks. I assumed he was with you, Morris said. But don't hang up—there's some terrible news about Ez. Somebody ran him over, killed him.

I freaked, of course. And said much more than I should have. Morris got just enough information out of me to put two and two together. He figured Jerry must've pulled some kind of robbery and Rube was in on it. That had to be the explanation, he said. Jerry must have double-crossed Rube. Killed him and then took off with his share of the score. We all know he's no angel, Morris said, but I never figured him for this horrible kind of thing.

No. No, neither did I.

I never saw Jerry again. He left me in a hell of a fix. I hated him for it. But I hated him more for what he'd done to Rube and for the part I'd played in destroying him. I knew I'd never get over it.

I stayed in Portugal for a while, long enough

to confirm I was pregnant. The way I had figured it, Jerry was going to be a proud dad and we were going to live the straight life and get a place in Barcelona, which we both loved, and grow old together.

Nope. The people at the little hotel where I was staying got me to the hospital one night. I lost the baby.

I had almost run out of money by then. I had to move on. I took any kind of work I could get. I lived in a few places in Germany for a while. Once or twice I even ran into people I knew in the old life. I always made an excuse for not spending any time with them. I lied about where and how I'd been living, and said I didn't want to go into my made-up "divorce" from Jerry. Then I'd move on quickly to someplace else. I lived like a kid hitch-hiking across Europe for the summer. I lived like a bum sometimes. Sometimes I'd meet a man who was just good enough, and not too curious about my past. I got along, and I didn't really think about it that much. It was just—just what my life had become.

This past winter, I thought I could risk being in France again. Enough time had passed to make me certain nobody was looking for me. I had a cheap room in the south and a job in a little boutique. My old friend Mimi came strolling in one day. She insisted I come to the house she and her boyfriend were renting. We caught up, kind of. Talked long into the night. It was Mimi who told me that Jerry was long dead; she couldn't believe I didn't know.

Didn't know he'd been found dead, murdered, at Orly Airport shortly after I left Paris. And it was real ugly how he died. She'd figured I split town because some guys Jerry was involved with had killed him and I was terrified they might kill me too.

Mimi told me something else. Maybe some of the others in our crowd knew it too. But nobody ever let it slip that Jerry had a wife and a kid back in the States. They figured he'd have to come clean and sort it out someday. But everybody knew, she said, that he adored me, that was what counted, and there was no way he would have ever abandoned me.

Funny, ain't it? Every-fucking-body loved Viv. Yet there was never anybody looking for me. And maybe that was the story of my life all along: I thought I was the brightest star in everybody's heaven, but nobody even blinked when I disappeared.

I laid a lot of crap on you and your man, a lot of lies. But believe me, I had my reasons. Forgive me forgive me please for not living up to your expectations. I'm just tired now, and sorry, and scared of dying, just like anybody else. The one thing I never wanted to be. Life is a bitch and then you die, right?

You'll never look up to me again baby. But please don't look down on me either. I love you Nan and I'm sorry.

We found that. But not the ten thousand dollars.

———————

ONE OF OUR street musician acquaintances had brought a keyboard by the apartment. Andre sat up in bed for hours on end, picking out tunes with one hand. He was going to be just fine. Andre did not appreciate being told that his wound was "not particularly serious," and in his place neither would I. Getting shot is by definition serious when it's your body the bullet has ripped through. But he did need to let the wound near his left nipple heal. Playing the violin would have to wait for at least a month. There was no reason he couldn't go outside if he took it easy, though . . . walk, sit in the café. He just didn't want to.

I fed him soup and gave him his antibiotics and, as if I weren't already guilty enough, broke his heart all over again every time we argued about me going back to New York. That argument seemed to take up about twenty out of every twenty-four hours. In the heat of the moment he called me a few names I knew he didn't mean, and so I never responded in kind.

"Look! I know you're deep into being Mr. Black Paris Exile. But for god's sake, baby, even Sidney Bechet came home once in a while—didn't he?"

"Stop calling it home, Nan."

"But it is."

"Bullshit. Home is someplace where you belong. Where you're wanted, and respected, and loved. Unconditionally. Home is where there's a place for you."

"I have a place for you, idiot. I have a home for you. We can work, Andre. We can get back here."

"To visit, you mean." He said it as though there was spoiled milk in his mouth. "Dabble, you mean. That's not me, Nanette. I'm not into vacationing. I want to belong. I'm for real."

"And I'm not? Just because I can see it's my place to take Viv's body home—be with my parents over this. I not only let her die alone, I threw away ten thousand dollars, man! I couldn't turn away from Viv while she was alive, and I can't turn away now."

"But from me you can. Right?"

"But I don't want to, my love. I don't want to."

"Well, you have to. Understand that. You have to either turn away from her or turn away from me."

After a while he just stopped talking. He put on a pair of blue-tinted wire-rim shades that just covered his eyeballs and sat there looking like a hippie CIA op.

I tried to play it for laughs. I tried reasoning with him. I tried to play it from every angle in the book. But he wasn't having it. I was "leaving him," that's how he saw it. "Leaving. Period." The silent treatment became his way of leaving me before I left him.

I knew how miserable he was. Because I knew how miserable I was.

When Inspector Simard phoned to say he was in Paris and wanted us to join him for lunch, I begged Andre to get dressed and come. But he wouldn't budge.

"I'm bringing back some ice cream for you," I told him as I slipped on my shoes and picked up the folding umbrella. "What flavor do you want? Pistachio?"

No answer.

"Come on, sweetheart. Please come. Simard wants to see you. He asked for you especially."

Nothing.

"You really hate me now, huh, Geechee?"

Nothing.

"Okay. Pistachio it is."

ÎLE SAINT-LOUIS IN THE RAIN. Notre-Dame hanging behind me in the mist like the fingers of an old hand pointing blackly up at God. There was a time when that would have given the old tear

ducts a workout. All out of tears now. There would be plenty of
time for them later. Never made love with Andre while it was
raining. How could that be?

Simard looked very snappy in his dark suit. He stood as I
approached the table, took my hands into his, looked into my
eyes for a long time. For a minute there I thought he might kiss
me. But no, he was an elderly man who had seen me only twice
in his life and that Gallic sense of reserve was too strong. Still, I
took note of the kindness in his eyes and was grateful for it.

I extended a fake apology on Andre's behalf for his absence,
and the meal commenced. The inspector of course did all the
ordering. The food was beautiful, and we put off talking about
the very reason he and I had ever crossed paths until the waiter
was clearing away the dishes.

"So," he said, "I read the copy of the letter your aunt left for
you. Thank you for sending it. The anguish in it was apparent.
And so was her feeling for you, her regret. It must have been
heartbreaking to read."

I nodded.

"At any rate, the autopsy has confirmed what she told you.
She was indeed gravely ill. There was an inoperable cancer of the
pancreas. One of the worst sorts, we all know that." He stopped
there, but a minute later added, "I've always said, when the day
comes that I'm given a similar diagnosis, I will most certainly
consider her way of . . ."

"Going out," I said, in English. "Yes, me too, I think. But in
a much quieter way."

I took a long drink from my—what?—third glass of wine.
"It's been mighty quiet lately in the apartment. I've had plenty
of time these past few days to try out a lot of answers to everything that Viv left unsaid.

"When she was holding Andre and me in that car, she told
us a series of lies. But, in her own way, she was telling the

truth at the same time. What I mean is, she laid out the cast of characters, and she provided a list of their actions—their betrayals, if you will. What I had to do was juggle the players—switch the names and faces and match them with the crimes committed."

"Please," Simard said. "I am eager to hear it."

"Couldn't make up his mind which side of the fence he was playing on. Viv said something like that. Let's assume that little Ez was quite drunk with being desired by this sexy lady *and* this very smart, sophisticated, charismatic older man."

"You mean Monsieur Melon."

"I certainly do. And now Ez-slash-Rube has made his choice. He's head over heels in love with Viv. And, at Jerry's urging, she makes him think she loves him, too. Even though she's married to Jerry."

"Not exactly, as Mademoiselle Mimi informed your aunt."

"Yeah. He's already taken, with a child in the picture as well."

I saw the inspector's eyes flick away from mine and back again.

"What?" I said. "You want to add something to that? What is it—he had five children? Five wives?"

"No, not at all. Go on."

"Vivian waits for Jerry. And waits. But he doesn't show, and he doesn't send for her. Slowly it begins to dawn on her that he never will. Meanwhile, poor Ez is brutally murdered. Vivian hears about it from Morris Melon. Now *there's* somebody who definitely knows which side of the sexual fence he's on; Melon is in love with Ez. And doesn't take it very well when Ez drops him. Around this time, there's a robbery—a casino, a safe in a rich person's home, maybe money that was earmarked for Jerry's underworld pals—I don't know. Perhaps Morris Melon suspects, or knows for sure, that it's Jerry who pulled off the job. And perhaps he even knows that Little Rube took part in the crime, too.

"At any rate, he is furious at Little Rube—at both of them,

really. So suppose he decides to whisper in the ears of Jerry's bad friends. *Maybe,* Melon is thinking, *they'll catch Jerry and Little Rube making a getaway and kill the both of them.* Sure enough, they do get Jerry, they do kill him, and of course they take the money. Melon decides to kill Little Rube himself."

"And perhaps takes money from him? After all, Monsieur Rube took part in the crime. He would have had a share. It probably added up to a good deal of money."

"Good point," I said. "In fact, an excellent point. Starting a business like Melon's requires dough. Now, any bets on who helped Morris Melon learn what was being planned, what crimes had occurred recently—robberies, for instance? Who'd be in a position to hear all kinds of chatter in low places, ready to sell information to whoever wanted to be in the know? What trifling scammer and snitch might figure into every part of this story?"

"Gigi Lacroix," the inspector said. "Of course. Lacroix."

"It's too perfect not to be."

"Meanwhile, your aunt is alone in Lisbon. Waiting and waiting. When she reaches out to Monsieur Melon, he tells her it's likely that her husband has run out on her *and* killed Rube."

"Yes. Now you come onstage, Inspector. You take the Rube Haskins murder seriously, pursue what leads you have. But unfortunately you don't find Rube's killer.

"The years pass. Morris Melon becomes a kind of elder statesman of the smart black set in Paris. Mister Bon Vivant. It's like he won a consolation prize; the person he loved rejected him, but life doesn't turn out so bad after all.

"Vivian gets on with her life, too. And all these years later, a chance meeting with an old friend named Mimi provides the shock of her life: Jerry didn't abandon her. He was about to get on a plane to join her in Lisbon. All those years with that heaviness, that hatred in her heart. She might even have had Jerry's child if things had gone as planned. It didn't take her long to look at the facts and come up with a damn good guess as to who's responsible for Jerry's death, and Rube's. Now she has a mission in life: to make Morris Melon pay.

"She's in Paris, and he knows it. He can't know for certain that she's figured everything out, but it's very likely. He strikes preemptively. When someone tries to kill her, there's no longer any doubt. Morris Melon is 'Satan.' Vivan's so spooked, she never returns to her hotel room.

"Then something truly satanic happens: a young woman— perhaps innocent—is killed, and Melon plans to implicate Viv in her death.

"But before Viv makes her move, there's another shock: she hears from a friend, somebody helping her lie low, that a young woman who claims to be her niece from New York is looking for her. She wants to know what on earth I'm doing here, why I'm trying to find her. Maybe it's a trap. But just maybe the family's worried about her and I've been sent to bail her out—which of course happens to be exactly right. But she can't just walk up to Andre and me. She's in danger; she's being hunted. So she stakes us out. She stalks us for a while.

"You know about her kidnapping Andre and her big confession to us in the back seat of the Volkswagen. Big lies, rather. But . . . are they?"

"Now," the inspector said, lighting my cigarette as well as his own, "I understand what you meant earlier, about the cast of characters. You said that what your aunt told you in the car was both true and false. She did indeed intend to kill this man from her past. To obtain her revenge. But the man was not Jerry Brainard; she was planning to kill Monsieur Melon."

"Right. And there's something else: it's the Mary Polk murder that convinces her Melon is trying to get her. She reads, just as Andre and I did, that the police had questioned and released a small-time criminal named Gigi Lacroix. One of the papers features a photograph of him. Vivian immediately remembers him from the old days. He's the man who tried to kill her outside the hotel. Not much Lacroix wouldn't do for money. Melon had hired him to kill her. That's when Viv really goes into hiding.

"But of course Nanette and her young lover don't know any of that. They walk right into the old man's net. He befriends them and sets them up with a part-time gig in his place, where he can track their progress just by keeping his ears open.

"And who does naive Nanette enlist to help find her aunt? A lifelong criminal who knows a little bit about a lot of things— Gigi Lacroix. The very hood who works as a strong-arm man, a snitch or whatever, for Morris Melon.

"Lacroix had great appreciation for the many jokes that life plays on us. He was taking money from me for the same service Melon was paying for—finding Vivian. 'Just string her along,' Melon probably told him. 'Take the cash she gives you and tell her as little as possible.'

"There was more irony than I knew what to do with, Inspector. For instance—the telegram that got sent to my mother. Morris Melon sent it. His man Gigi must have gotten his hands on Viv's address book when he rifled through her hotel room. Melon sent that telegram asking for money, hoping somebody from the family would come over here and flush Vivian out. It was a long shot for him. But Satan seems to have had all the luck, you know? I actually did have a jackpot for her."

Simard did his duty as taster when the waiter opened yet another bottle of wine. He nodded his approval, and our glasses were filled. We drank in silence for a time.

————

"I KNOW HOW useless hindsight is," I commented later. "But, thinking back on all of it, I realize how plain some of these things should have been to me. Viv called him Satan.

"*Big* mistake, my not picking up on that one. I mean, Jerry sounds like he could be a son of a bitch at times, but . . . Satan? No. On the other hand, it's not hard to imagine charming, welcoming, funny Monsieur Melon having a dark side, an evil side. He must have started out on the side of the angels, but then once he slipped—once he found he was actually capable of murdering Rube Haskins, someone he loved—he figured he had to go all the way to the other end of morality—to being a devil. I remember how he talked about the blessedness of black people from the country. *Grace* was the word he used. When he turned, it was like he was stomping on the grace of his people and renouncing his own blessedness. He wasn't just killing people; he was killing his shame. Ez. Jerry. Mary Polk. Then Vivian, very nearly."

"And Gigi Lacroix?" Simard said. "Are you forgetting him, or don't you believe Melon murdered him, too? He did have a motive—speculatively, anyway."

"Did he? Oh, oh sure. You're right, Melon could have been making sure Gigi would never be able to inform on him."

"Yes," Simard said. "I do mean that. You never discovered why he called you that evening and told you to come meet him in Les Halles."

"No, I didn't. He was dead when we got there."

"*Oui.* And I am imagining he had some ten thousand reasons for wanting to see you. If he managed to find out what you had for your aunt, he was greedy enough to try to get it. Of course Melon dispatched Lacroix to kill your aunt. But look at the number of times Gigi botched that assignment. He made a very poor hit man.

"I believe Gigi is not the prime suspect in the other murders,"

Simard continued. "I say that, with careful planning, Melon might very well have personally carried out the murder of Mary Polk. Who can say, even, that he did not follow Jerry Brainard to the airport and kill him all those years ago?

"Melon knew who he was dealing with in Gigi. As to why he felt he must get rid of Lacroix at that moment? He suspected Lacroix was on the verge of trying to sell you some real information for a change—some things much too dangerous for you to know. He'd have told you the complete saga, going all the way back to Melon's betrayal of Jerry and Rube. He thought maybe you would agree to send Martine to get the money while you and he waited on that park bench. Then, when she returned with it, he'd tell you everything."

"But Morris was in the club when Gigi was killed at Les Halles," I said. "He had a dreadful hangover and . . . I see. Yeah, he went into his office and put himself to bed. You're saying he was bull—I mean, pretending."

Simard nodded. "Yes, he pretended to be ill with a hangover. He retired to his private office to sleep. But while you and Andre and the others performed, he slipped out and simply made the short walk to the Métro. He joined Lacroix in the square, sat quite close to him as they talked, and soundlessly drove the knife into his body. He returned to Bricktop's and slipped in the back entrance, and no one was any the wiser."

"I don't know," I said. "I'm a fan of the much simpler explanation: Viv did it.

"I asked my aunt a question as she was driving away: 'What do you need that money for?' Viv knew she didn't have a chance of escaping after killing Melon. She didn't answer me then, and now those money orders have vanished. What did she do with them? God knows I'd love to be able to answer that question when my mother asks it.

"As for Jerry Brainard—you know what I'm starting to

believe about him, Inspector? Wrong guy that he was? That he cared for Vivian almost as much as she did for him. That he was a weak man, always in trouble, always in debt. He stole because it was the simplest way to get what he needed. I wonder if he didn't find himself at gunpoint in that car, seconds from death, and suddenly realize he'd have been better off staying with Viv and working for a living like everybody else."

Simard smiled ruefully. "And what about Haskins?" he said. "What was, in your estimation, his driving need?"

"His need was for Vivian, I suppose. Poor bastard."

"Poor bastard," the inspector echoed. "You've cast a very forgiving eye on all the players in your drama, you know. Mysteries or no mysteries, I could never look at them with the kind of pity you do. But tell me this: Are you purposely leaving one character out of this complicated tale of expatriates?"

"Who would that be?"

"Yourself, my friend."

Me? Sure, I could toss around some ideas about what drives me. But I did much better speculating, piecing together the motivations of four dead people. Who weren't around to tell me I was full of shit.

I merely shrugged.

We'd been lunching for three and a half hours. I had to get back to the rue Christine.

"I take it," Monsieur Simard said as I walked him to his taxi, "that you and Andre . . ." He allowed his voice to simply drop off the cliff there.

I shook my head, not trusting myself to speak.

"Ah." That was all he said. But the word seemed to come from deep in his chest.

"Nanette," he said a few minutes later. It startled me. It was the first time he had called me by my first name.

"*Oui?*"

"About the cruel murder of Mary Polk."

"Oh yes, I thought you looked funny when her name was mentioned. What about her?"

"I asked myself if I should tell you. Because you have enough . . ."

I didn't speak. I just waited.

"I've decided you should know. Better to send you home with all the sad things at once." He sighed before going on. "Mary Polk was Jerry Brainard's daughter. She was in Paris looking for her father."

I couldn't speak for a few minutes. All I could do was nod slowly.

It was a long while before he spoke again. "You loved your aunt, did you not? And you believe that, despite the unhappy turn her life took, she loved you as well?"

I nodded.

"I think, Nanette, you must accept that everyone is entitled to their mysteries. But perhaps there is a very practical answer to what Vivian did with the bulk of that ten thousand dollars."

I looked at him expectantly.

"If Rube Haskins was so completely taken with her, he probably told her who he really was. She may have known his real name, where he was born, everything."

"Yes, I guess that makes sense."

"What was that phrase you used . . . payback? Too little, and too late. But a kind of payback."

"What is it you're not telling me, Monsieur Simard?"

"The clerk who sold postage to your aunt remembered her because she looked ill. As if she had a fever. The day after she left you and Andre standing in Cité Prost, your aunt Vivian sent a large envelope by air to the United States. That is all the young lady at the post office recalled."

Ah. So maybe Vivian had made a last-ditch attempt to redress the wrong she had done Ez. She had sent her inheritance to his family. Or maybe back to my mom.

I kissed the inspector then. I couldn't help myself. "I'll write to you," I said.

"Excellent. I haven't had a good letter in ten years."

"And will you?" I asked.

"The minute anything interesting occurs."

I FORGOT the ice cream.

Just as well.

Andre was gone.

> Nan:
> Go. Leave keys downstairs. Go Go I won't come
> back till you do.

I packed in a hurry, to say the least, so I'm sure I must have left something behind. If so, I didn't do it on purpose. Believe me.

Ah, I thought, there was a cue I didn't pick up on. Before I left the apartment to join Simard, Andre was playing around with that keyboard. He was playing something kitschy—Viennese—something like "Fascination." But as the little lift descended, I could have sworn I heard the opening notes to Gordon Jenkins's "Goodbye."

CHAPTER 17

LONG AGO AND FAR AWAY

VIVIAN SIGHED, *blowing out a beautiful purple plume. "Nobody gives a better foot rub than you, darling."*

Jerry kissed a couple of her toes. "And nobody has feet as beautiful as yours. How about a hit of that?"

He pulled himself up onto the bed, took a mighty pull from the joint, then enfolded her in his arms. "Nervous?"

"Yes."

"You shouldn't be. We got it covered. You just get yourself to the hotel, order some nice champagne. Go for a swim or something. Just cool it, and I'll be there in a couple of days. And tell all the handsome Portuguese men that you're taken."

Vivian closed her eyes for a moment. Don't say anything, she told herself. Not yet. Anyway, you're not sure yet. Only a couple weeks late. And if it's true, he might even be happy about it.

Viv wasn't so happy about leaving Paris, but she knew they had to—for a while, anyway. Jerry would be "hot." Even without knowing the details of what he and Ez were going to do, she knew they'd need to get out of town.

Vivian and Jerry remained in their position for a long time: her in his arms, both of them quiet. She finally broke the silence. "We're ridiculous. You know that, right?"

He laughed. "I beg your pardon. What's ridiculous about us?"

"Everything. At the moment I'm thinking of the dumbass hoax you and Morris were trying to pull off with Ez. Passing him off as a blues legend. I can't believe you really thought that was going to fly with that idiot producer."

"He had a shitload of his daddy's money and a gigantic habit. And, like you said, he was an idiot. It might have worked . . . maybe."

"Not in a thousand years, dummy. All three of you were doing way too much speed last year."

"Yeah. I know. And after this job . . . well, never mind about that. We're going to live a clean life from here on out."

"Um-hum."

"No, I mean it, babe. We cool it in Lisbon for a while, then we get this great place in Barcelona that my man Bobby owns. Ez'll wait it out in Italy and then he'll join us. Happy family again, right?"

Vivian held tight to Jerry's arm.

"What?" He kissed her fingers. "Don't you be scared. Like you said, I am kind of ridiculous. And I can't believe you could love a moron like me. But this thing is solid. I'm gonna make you so fucking happy. Like, forever."

"You already do. I just keep thinking, what if—"

"What if nothing. I love you."

"Happy family again, eh?"

"That's right."

He began to push the straps of her gown off her shoulders.

"Hmm," she said, "about Barcelona. You and me and Ez. How big is that bed?"

"Oh, it's big."

———

MORRIS MELON WORE *polka-dot pajamas. He was not a happy man today. He paced the shearling rug, halting from time to time to speak directly into Ez's face.*

"What makes you think you can just pick up and leave? You'll never manage on your own. You may think you know the world just because women like that thing between your legs. But you're nothing but a big baby."

Ez lit a cigarette and made a big show of blowing out the match. From his place on the love seat, he looked up and smiled at Morris.

"Such ingratitude. Where would you be if I hadn't taken you in?"

"You ain't taken me no place, Morris."

"I introduced you to le tout Paris, *didn't I? To everyone who counts, that is. You had no idea how to dress or behave or command a meal or—"*

"Put powder up my nose. You wanted me to pay you back for civilizing me, Morris? I think by now you got your money's worth."

"That's a vulgar thing to say."

"So I'm still vulgar. That ain't something I hear you complain about most of the time."

"It's an open secret, you know—your special friendship with Vivian. With Vivian and her husband, that is. People talk."

"Let 'em talk. What's that thing you always used to say? 'If you ain't news, you're nothin'.' I'm not in the church choir no more. And you ain't been there for a long, long time. I don't think you miss it any more than I do."

"You really believe you're a sophisticate, don't you? Let me tell you— Jerry and Viv will use you until they use you up. It isn't even their fault, really. They're shallow people, too beautiful for their own good. I warn you: throw in with Jerry and we'll be burying you—well, you'll hardly rate Père Lachaise, but you'll be in a pauper's grave faster than you can blink. I won't be attending any service. I'll be here, laughing, drinking wine you can't even pronounce. 'Rube.' If ever a name fit the man owning it."

"Look, Mo, in a couple of hours you gonna think about what you doing now and come begging my forgiveness. You know it. Why don't you do it now and let's be friends again."

Morris turned suddenly, eyes bright with hope. "You're right," he said. "And will you give it me? You know I only said those things because I don't want you to go."

"I'm going," Ez said.

Oh no, thought Morris. You're not.

CHAPTER 18

PARTING IS NOT GOOD-BYE

I WROTE A NOTE, TOO. On the back of the one he'd left for me. But in the end I didn't leave it.

I had it in my purse.

What am I doing here?

I belonged with Andre, didn't I? He was the one who was so caught up with "belonging" to a place. Not me, not anymore. I was beginning to accept that I'd always be a little bit on the periphery. Fuck the *place*—it was Andre I belonged with, no? So what was I doing up above the world, heading back to America? Alone.

You're taking Vivian's body home. That's what you're doing. Her brother is going to bury her, and maybe you along with her.

To repeat, I belonged with Andre, didn't I? Here was a man who had not only pledged the rest of his life to me. Not only could play "Billie's Bounce" on the violin. Not only showed a willingness to face down my shitty karma. He loved me enough to take a bullet that by all rights should have been mine.

"Madame?" I heard a soft voice say.

The flight was only half full. The attendant with the chignon wouldn't leave me alone. I had already declined the game hen dinner, smoked salmon, honey peanuts, champagne, current issue of *Paris Vogue*, and in-flight Julia Roberts movie. With each offer I turned my puffy, ugly old face to her and tried to answer in the fewest polite French words possible.

I had downed an ocean of black coffee since boarding the plane.

The poison gas began to rise again in my stomach as I had another flashback of Vivian lying in that alley with her face blown off.

I turned on the overhead light to help chase the image away.

I lived too much in the past. That was my trouble. That's what the music was about, when you really got down to it. It wasn't just what I did for a half-assed living, what I respected and loved. It was my escape from the world as presently constituted.

Worse, it wasn't even *my* past. All my life it seems I've been caught up with the people, the music, and the feel of life at another time, a time at least three generations removed from my own. Here you are, little Nanette, it's 1969 and here's the gift of life. Welcome to the world, dear. What are you going to be, a postal worker, a bank manager—you know, they let us do that kind of thing now—or a computer whiz? *Me? Thanks, but no thanks. I'd rather be Mary Lou Williams. Ivy Anderson? Or, yeah, how about Sonny Rollins?* I could never get with the music I was supposed to like. Nor the kind of man I was supposed to like. Nor the kinds of ambitions that were supposed to drive me forward. I don't give a damn about the things that excite or tie up the folks drinking shooters on the Upper West Side or hanging with Spike in Fort Greene.

Yes, through the music of the past I had, like Andre, found a way to honor my forefathers. But I knew there was something terribly dishonest about the way I lived. It wasn't just living in a fantasy world, it wasn't just being phony—it was wrong. It's wrong not to live in the here and now. It's cowardly and pious and arrogant and wrong.

And the other kids just don't like me.

If I played my cards right I could spend the whole flight beating up on myself. I think it must have been Ernestine—that voice in my ear that was telling me: *If you feel this awful, you must deserve it.*

Pictures of Andre were now interspersed with the memories of Vivian. Those big feet of his, and the way he moved, and that hollow place in his lower back. The day he took me on that breathless guided tour, the same day we first went to Bricktop's. Teasing him then, I said he was mad—that his devotion to the past had screwed him up. Well, maybe that was no joke; maybe he *was* genuinely mad, for real. And, finally, those cold blue killer-for-hire shades that obscured his eyes, hid him, took him from me during the last days we had together.

Belong with him? said Ernestine scornfully. *You'll never see him again.*

It wasn't fair, it wasn't fair.

I dug a few paper napkins out of the seat-back pocket and dabbed at my eyes.

Would Andre continue to live and work in Paris, stay on in France forever? He sure had the talent and the determination. I had no doubt he would do our forebears proud, the obscure ones along with the famous. All those black people with a hyper-developed sense of the romantic that takes them to faraway places, out of the here and now they were born to endure in America. Maybe someday, as maturity softened his contempt, he'd be able to view Aunt Vivian in a more sympathetic light. And Morris Melon. And me. All us permanent strangers.

Sure, Andre would distinguish himself in print or as a venerable lecturer or an acclaimed performer. He'd get—I made myself say it—get married, become a French citizen, like he wanted, and grow into his Inspector Simard role. A stone cottage in the provinces, two dogs—the whole bit. *Un homme français.*

The aircraft shimmied a little and then the pilot's reassuring baritone issued from the loudspeaker. In a nutshell: *Go back to sleep, it's going to be okay.*

Would I ever see Paris again? Probably. It was unbearable to think of dying without seeing those lights once more. Would I ever cry again as I drove past the Arc de Triomphe or walked in the Bois de Boulogne? Maybe. Would I ever again feel that the city belonged to me, and I to it? Like I wasn't just another savvy tourist, or even a starry-eyed expatriate, but the genuine article—*une femme française?*

No.

Read More
Nanette Hayes Mysteries
by Charlotte Carter

RHODE ISLAND RED
Book One

Meet jazz-loving street busker
Nanette, who begins a hunt for
a legendary saxophone worth
its weight in gold—only to find
that there are plenty of people
willing to kill for it.

DRUMSTICKS
Book Three

Nan finds a voodoo doll that
brings her some much-needed
luck . . . until the doll's maker
is murdered and Nan is dragged
into the investigation.